Turning to face her, Grant met her troubled green eyes squarely. 'You're not going to like what I have to say, Anne.'

Her manner lightened. 'You can't make the charity ball . . . is that it?'

'No, not that. I'll come to your ball. But I want to make it plain from the outset how we stand.'

'What are you driving at?' Anne returned, wide-eyed, her stomach lurching.

'Look, let's be honest about this . . .' He scratched his head with a kind of despair. 'I know and *you* know that we're . . . well, mutually attracted, for want of a better description. But I have to spell it out . . . there's no future in it.'

'Aren't you taking a lot for granted?' she retorted. 'Yes, of course I like you or I wouldn't be here. But, as I told your foster-mother, we're just friends.'

'Fine! And that's how it has to stay, because our ways of life are totally incompatible.'

Grace Read has had a life-long love affair with nursing. Starting as a Red Cross Nurse in a London hospital during the war, she went on to do her general training in the Midlands. Marriage and a baby ended that career, but she retains a keen interest in the profession. She has a son and two daughters. Her youngest daughter is a nursing sister and keeps 'Mum' abreast of modern trends, vetting her novels for medical accuracy. When she is not writing Grace enjoys gardening, travelling to research backgrounds, and admits to a fondness for golden Labradors.

Previous Titles

DR DRUMMOND ADVISES
TIDES OF THE HEART
CASUALTIES OF LOVE

THE HUMAN TOUCH

BY

GRACE READ

MILLS & BOON LIMITED
ETON HOUSE   18-24 PARADISE ROAD
RICHMOND   SURREY   TW9 1SR

*First published in Great Britain 1989
by Mills & Boon Limited*

© Grace Read 1989

*Australian copyright 1989
Philippine copyright 1989
This edition 1990*

ISBN 0 263 76694 2

*Set in Times 12 on 12 pt.
03 – 9001 – 44789*

Typeset in Great Britain by JCL Graphics, Bristol

Made and Printed in Great Britain

CHAPTER ONE

COMPARED with the heatwave in which London was basking during that third week of June, the temperature in the operating theatre at St Martin's Hospital was comfortably controlled. All the same, Circulating Nurse Anne Westlake, swathed in shapeless theatre gown and mask, her fair hair piled beneath a floral cap, felt near to melting point. And the nature of the operation in progress didn't help as she flitted on silent feet performing her many duties.

A critical part in the craniotomy had now been reached. The team clustered around the patient on the table as Grant Ryder, rising young neurosurgeon, located the bleeding point in the wealthy businessman's brain.

'A textbook berry aneurysm . . .' the surgeon murmured with satisfaction. 'We should be able to clip this all right. Thank you, Sister.' He held out a gloved hand and Sister Miriam O'Connor passed him the required device.

Having completed his sealing of the ruptured vessel, the surgeon paused, eased his broad shoulders and glanced up. 'Anyone else like to have a look before we get on?' His discerning blue eyes caught sight of Anne standing by the swab-count rack. 'How about you, Nurse? It isn't every day you can get to see inside the head of a financial wizard.'

Anne smiled behind her mask, although privately giving vent to a very unladylike expression. Impressed though she was by the new surgeon's competent performance, she had been doing her best to distance herself from the action. She was not in love with the brass-tacks end of surgery and was heartily glad that this would be her last session in theatre. The sound of the bone-cutting instruments removing a flap of Alistair Carle's skull had been stomach-churning enough without her having to view the contents.

Nevertheless, she could scarcely refuse the invitation. Approaching as bidden, Anne suppressed a shudder as she peered into the mass of matter which makes mankind so different from other warm-blooded creatures.

Cheerfully Grant Ryder pointed out the leaking sac he had isolated and the cerebral arteries of which it was part. 'The circle of Willis, you see? A congenital weakness in the wall, here. Everything else looks healthy enough. Barring the unpredictable, this fellow should do well once he's over the trauma.'

'Terrific,' Anne said compliantly. Their eyes met briefly over their masks—his, intensely blue and appraising under straight dark brows; hers, green and long-lashed, expressing polite interest with a hint of devilment.

'I'll keep my fingers crossed for him,' she murmured, and removed herself so that the operating team could get on with their task of closing the wound.

'Crossed fingers won't get him very far. I'd prefer some skilled aftercare to supplement my efforts,' Grant Ryder said with a touch of irony, returning to his task.

'Oh, he'll get that as well.' Sister Miriam supplied the piece of drainage tube he asked for. 'Crossed fingers is a bonus from our nurses, Mr Ryder.'

Georges Alain, the dark-eyed French anaesthetist, winked in Anne's direction. 'So now she also 'as a bonus. She knows what goes on inside a man's 'ead, *hein*?' he teased.

'If it were *that* simple I'd have had my husband on the table long ago,' Miriam rejoined.

Sharon, the other scrub nurse, rolled her eyes at Anne. Anne smothered a giggle and carried on with her own work of removing discarded swabs, replacing bowls of saline and supplying whatever else was required.

The operation successfully concluded and instruments and swabs checked and accounted for, the patient was transferred to the care of the recovery-room staff. Anne pulled off her mask and gown and went out to ensure that coffee would be ready for them all after what had been a taxing afternoon.

In the rest-room, stripped of their gowns, the doctors relaxed, their conversation revolving around the lifestyle of the patient. Besides being a high-powered financier, Alistair Carle owned a number of racehorses. It was the excitement of seeing one of them win at an Ascot meeting which had brought on the brain haemorrhage for which he had just been treated.

'Wish I'd had some money on that horse of his,' Senior Houseman Bob Ramsgate reflected, stirring his coffee. 'Basis Oasis came home at twenty to one, so I was told.'

'What a ridiculous name!' scoffed Sister Miriam, removing the clingfilm from a plate of sandwiches on the coffee table. 'What would you call a horse if you had one, Mr Ryder?'

The neurosurgeon, his lean limbs easy in blue cotton singlet and trousers, stretched full-length in a low chair and smoothed his rumpled dark hair with well-kept hands. 'Not something I've thought about, since I'm never likely to own one. I just concentrate on patching up the people who go bananas when they back a loser.'

'Never had a flutter?' Bob pushed his gold-rimmed spectacles further on his nose and eyed his new boss warily, wondering if he'd stumbled on a delicate subject. After all, as yet nobody knew much about this man except that he was back in England after working and lecturing in America for a year.

Grant Ryder shook his head. He pursed his lips and blew lightly to cool his coffee before answering. 'Too much respect for my hard-earned cash, Bob. The racing world may be fine for the rich, but lives can be ruined when people get hooked on gambling and they can't afford it. Addictive, isn't it, like drugs or drink?'

There followed a free-for-all on gambling in general. Anne didn't join in. She stayed in the background with her coffee, then quietly disappeared to get on with cleaning up in the theatre. First because she was in a hurry to get away that evening, and secondly because talk about the haves and have-nots always made her feel uncomfortable. Coming from a privileged background, and with a sizeable legacy left her by her grandfather when she was twenty-one, she had never felt the pinch like some of her nursing friends having to exist on their student pay.

When she had made up her mind to train as a nurse her entire family thought she must be mad, or at least that she would come to her senses after a month or two. At the time not even her sister Michelle had known of her hopeless obsession with the Hon. Jonathan Locke, already married and with two children. Jonathan owned the art gallery where Anne had worked. To enter nursing gave her at least a logical reason for escaping. In the eyes of the family, however, to abandon a socially acceptable occupation in congenial surroundings was quixotic, to say the least.

'A *nurse*?' Michelle exclaimed in amusement when Anne made known her plans soon after her twenty-first birthday party at the Café Royal. 'I don't believe it! Grandfather's money must have gone to your head!'

Her mother sighed, 'Oh dear! I suppose this is a result of having your appendix out last year. You'll find it a very different matter from being a patient at the Cromwell, Anne. And I think it's most inconsiderate of you to let Jonathan down.'

'Well, the truth is I'm bored to death at the Gallery,' Anne had explained. 'It has nothing to do with noble motives or anything like that. I simply want a challenging job, one that really extends me. Nurses are always in short supply, aren't they? And Jon won't have any difficulty in replacing me.'

Her father, who believed in letting people do their own thing so long as it didn't inconvenience him, patted her on the head indulgently. 'Have a go by all means, my dear,' he said. 'You can always drop out when we find you a husband.'

All of which made Anne determined to succeed. And four years later she had. At twenty-five she was now a staff nurse and couldn't have been happier. Her original thinking had been that hard work and study would get Jonathan out of her system, once she had removed herself from his orbit. It came as a wonderful surprise to find herself completely captivated by her new career.

From the very beginning she had loved the feeling of belonging that had built up among the girls in her set. They were a cross-section from all walks of life, but the common bond of their work overcame all barriers.

To start with, living in the nurses' home had been a wise decision for Anne, since it put her on the same footing as everyone else. Recently, though, she and Mandy Green had branched out to share a flat a stone's throw from the hospital. It was the ground floor of a shabby old house, the upper floor of which was occupied by a houseman and his girlfriend, with whom they got on well. After three years of communal living the girls were revelling in their new-found freedom.

The memory of Jonathan Locke had long since faded from Anne's mind. In fact, when glancing through the gossip columns she had seen the announcement of the birth of his third child, Anne realised with a start that she hadn't thought about Jonathan for ages. She was glad she'd had the courage to make the break when she did. He was the eternal charmer, and his married status was no deterrent. And it was not one he had any intention of changing. Anne had long ago realised that.

'Hey, what's the mad rush?' queried Sharon, joining Anne in the theatre some ten minutes later. 'There's nothing else booked for today. That was the last op.'

'And my last op. altogether!' crowed Anne, bagging the used gowns for sterilisation. 'I start my Neurology course on Monday.'

Sharon's eyes widened in her round brown face. 'Oh, Neuro . . . so you'll be seeing a lot more of Ryder. Seems OK, doesn't he?' She began, in a leisurely fashion, to check and pack up the instruments for return to the Central Sterilising Department, humming a current pop song quietly to herself.

'Yeah! So far, so good,' Anne agreed. 'Seems to have strong views on some things, though,' she went on, busy emptying bowls and disinfecting surfaces. 'He might not be too easy to get along with . . .'

'Oh, you mean all that stuff about gambling. Well, he's right,' Sharon nodded. 'I mean, those amusement arcades, for instance, they're just machines for eating money, as my mum's always telling my kid brother, for all the good it does. The saucy monkey turns round and accuses her of spending the housekeeping on bingo! You coming over to the Friars for a bevvy when we've finished here?'

'Sorry, Sharon, got a date. Only with my dad.' Anne laughed as the other girl's eyes livened with curiosity. 'He's taking me and my sister to the Barbican—belated birthday treat.'

'Oh, what's on there?'

'Music—the Royal Philharmonic and Kiri Te Kanawa.'

'Oh! I'd sooner hear Michael Jackson meself,' said Sharon.

As it happened, Anne's companions that evening were not quite whom she expected. Taking a taxi to the Centre, she found her father waiting on the Waterside Terrace as arranged; a distinguished-looking man with thick silvering hair, his ex-Guards bearing still very evident. Immaculate in a black dinner jacket, he greeted her fondly, his eyes registering approval at her appearance.

She wore a simple but stylish frock in black crêpe de Chine which draped flatteringly about her slender figure. Her jewellery was a gold necklet and gold pendant earrings, while her lustrous blonde hair swung lightly about her creamy bare shoulders.

'Hello, my dear. You look a million dollars, as they say,' he remarked amiably.

'And so do you,' she returned, smiling. They kissed dutifully. 'I've beaten Michelle to it, have I? Thought I was the one who would be late. I had to put my skates on.'

'Ah! Michelle had to cry off at the last moment,' Sir Randolph Westlake said, 'but the seat won't be wasted. I bumped into your ex-employer at the club.'

'You mean Jon?' Her heart suddenly missed a beat.

'Yes—his wife's just given him another son. He was complaining that he felt surplus to requirements at home. I thought you might quite like to see him again.'

'Oh—er, yes,' said Anne. 'Do you know, I've not set eyes on him since I left the Gallery?'

'Yes, so he mentioned, somewhat regretfully, I thought. You should try to keep in touch with old friends, my dear. You never know when you might need them. He may be a little late, so we'll go in and have a drink, shall we?' Putting a hand under her elbow, he guided her towards the carpeted concourse thronging with people going in various directions. 'I said we'd be at the Stalls Bar if he should arrive in time,' her father added, making for the broad staircase overhung by the enormous sculptured lighting piece.

Anne shelved for the moment her annoyance at the turn of events and her reluctance even to see Jon again. It had been bound to happen some day, she supposed, and better with others present than on her own.

'So what's Michelle up to?' she asked.

'Researching something for her Current Affairs programme—taking some actor fellow out to dinner. Her TV career certainly seems to have taken off since she left Dominic, which is just as well. It stops her moping. But I wish she'd slow up a bit. She seems to be perpetually at the double.' Sir Randolph paused as they approached the bar. 'Dry Martini, is it?'

'Yes, please, Daddy.' Anne watched while he eased his way to the front of the bar and waited to be served. There was a certain air of resignation about his demeanour which saddened her—as though life of late had wearied him. She wished she could show him how much she loved him, but he was a reserved man who did not encourage displays of affection.

The last two years had been tough on them as a family, and especially so for her father. There had been the tragedy of her mother's death from a riding accident. It has happened shortly after Michelle's big wedding to Dominic. The marriage, which their mother had taken such delight in arranging, lasted barely nine months before Michelle was back in tears at the family house in Kensington. She had left Dominic and she was never going back to him, she pronounced, between paroxysms of weeping. When she could talk coherently it transpired that it was Dominic who had left Michelle and gone to live with his male lover.

Anne was glad that at least her father had no inkling of how she had felt about Jonathan Locke. It would have been an added trial to him had she become involved in an unsavoury affair. While she had been working at the Gallery Jon had made no secret of his liking for her. She resolved to be on her guard tonight to give him no encouragement.

Nostalgia about times past mingled with a certain pity for her lonely father. Impulsively she gave him a warm smile and kissed his cheek when he brought her the drink.

There were a number of people that evening who gave more than a passing glance towards the pleasant young girl and her mature escort. One of them was an American doctor staying for a time with Grant Ryder who had worked with him in New York.

'She's a stunner!' Brad Stevens murmured. 'No doubt about it, Grant, your English girls take some beating. But he's too old for her, wouldn't you say?' He sighed. 'Money talks, I guess.'

Grant Ryder had also been looking and wondering what it was about the girl that gave him a *déjà vu* kind of feeling. Then the image clicked when she inclined her head in a certain way. 'I know her,' he said, 'but when I saw her she didn't look like that. She was the runner in theatre while

I was operating today. Said she'd keep her fingers crossed for my patient, the cheeky puss!'

Brad Stevens laughed. 'Say, how about introducing me? Or do you think she believes in keeping her legs crossed as well?'

It was a remark that struck a discordant note with Grant, and he certainly had no intention of making introductions, even if he knew the girl's name, which he didn't. 'When I said I *knew* her I only meant that I'd seen her, and I wouldn't dream of crashing in on her date,' he said, glancing at his watch. 'Time we took our seats, Brad.'

Tension had been building in Anne as they waited for Jonathan Locke to join them. She couldn't really tell how she was going to feel on seeing him. How much would he have changed with the passing years? He would be in his early forties now and with any luck more responsible since the birth of his third child. Although leopards never changed their spots, did they?

She herself had changed, she knew. She was less impressionable and more given to careful judgements now. Her training over the past four years had taught her to think and improved her self-confidence. Indeed, she could look back on those early days and wonder how she could ever have been so stupid as to mistake an adolescent crush for love. All the same there remained that tiny seed of uncertainty—the unpredictable—as Grant Ryder had called it earlier that day.

Jonathan arrived as Anne and her father were about to make their way to the Concert Hall. There was little time for anything but the briefest of greetings and enquiries about his wife and the new baby before the performance began. But Anne found to her relief that she need not have worried. He was still the same smooth-tongued Jon, with the gift of making a woman feel special, but she could recognise it for what it was—a highly polished performance. She could enjoy his attentions without the slightest danger of falling overboard.

Anne settled down contentedly between her two stylish escorts, all set to enjoy the concert. Records were well enough, but there was nothing to match a live performance.

'Is this up your street, then?' Jon murmured in her ear as she clapped enthusiastically at the end of the Overture to *Don Giovanni.*

She turned to smile at him. His thick brown hair, she noted, had begun to recede a little. 'Yes. Why, isn't it yours?'

He gave an airy gesture and grinned wickedly. 'It's *you* I really came to see. I was interested to see how you'd grown up.'

'I was grown up when you last saw me!' she protested.

'Perhaps I should have said,' Jon paused, eyeing her teasingly, 'to see whether the promising bud had unfolded to the perfect blossom. And it has.'

She giggled. 'Good gracious! Does Mozart always have this effect on you . . . or is this some kind of neonatal afterglow?'

He sighed. 'Feeling my years after spawning my third son might be a more accurate description. I was hoping for a daughter this time.' He leaned across to speak to Anne's father. 'You're a lucky chap, having two decorative daughters. I'm not giving up, though. I shall try again.'

'Poor Belinda!' Anne sympathised.

'Oh, she doesn't mind. She revels in the production line,' Jon returned. 'Anyway, it leaves a chap plenty of time for his own pursuits.'

After the concert they dined at the Savoy, with both men showing a keen interest in Anne's present lifestyle.

'She could easily commute from Kensington,' her father said, 'but she prefers a hovel in some dingy quarter of the City to the comforts of home.'

'It's not a hovel,' laughed Anne, 'but I'm not a nine-thirty-to-five person these days, so it's more convenient to be on the spot. Anyway, I've lost touch with the old crowd. Even Mich and I don't have the same mutual interests as we did.' She used her sister's nickname.

'Speaking of old friends, Randolph,' Jon put in, 'I hear Alistair Carle collapsed at Ascot the other day. Apoplexy after a big win, so the story goes. Heard how he is?'

'Alistair Carle?' Anne frowned. 'We operated on a man of that name today, for a brain haemorrhage. If it's the same person, the surgeon was optimistic about the outcome.'

'Oh, so he's in St Martin's? Splendid! I may call and see him if he's up to receiving visitors. I could look you up at the same time, couldn't I?' Jon suggested.

'We-ell, I'm starting a new course on Monday, so I may be up to my ears in lectures,' Anne told him. Not that she was afraid of her feelings any more. Getting to know some of life's real victims during her training had taught her what suffering really was.

'You're still studying?' said Jon in disbelief. He eyed her modest curves. 'You'll never make Matron. Wrong vital statistics, Anne.'

Her father smiled drily. 'I'm keeping my eyes open for a suitable partner for her when she's got this out of her system. I need some grandchildren. Michelle seems to have opted out on that score— too busy with her career.'

'Anne could always come back to the Gallery. We have a promising breed of patrons passing through,' Jon reminded her, cradling his brandy and casting her a sideways glance.

She patted a polite yawn. 'If you've both finished deciding what I'm to do with the rest of my life . . . it has been a very long day.'

'Yes, of course,' agreed her father. 'Drink up, Jon.'

Anne draped her colourful scarf about her shoulders and they stepped out into the cool, velvet-black night. She stood for a moment savouring the summer-scented air, while the commissionaire hailed them a taxi.

Across the wide thoroughfare, beyond the cruising traffic and below the Embankment strung with its lighted garlands, London's river flowed darkly and silently. Anne thought with sudden pity of the ragged bundles of London's homeless who would be sheltering in dark doorways or stretched out on park benches, seeking escape in sleep.

Some of those unfortunates might already have been through her hands when she'd been on duty in St Martin's Casualty. Summer nights were not so bad, but she wondered how many of them would survive a hard winter, and once more she felt guilty for her own comfortable upbringing. It eased her conscience a little to know that she was working usefully for her living.

Jonathan planned to spend the night at his club in Piccadilly. After dropping him there the taxi carried Anne and her father on towards their home in Kensington. Lights glowed from the windows of the gracious period house in the quiet square. A familiar white Triumph convertible sat parked by the garden railings opposite.

'Ah! Michelle's home.' Sir Randolph paid off the taxi. 'Splendid. So I can go off to my golf tomorrow with a clear conscience. You two don't need me around, do you?'

Anne smiled. 'You know we love to have you around, but that's OK, Mich and I can amuse ourselves.'

Together they went up the small flight of steps to the porticoed entrance and in at the handsome oak front door with its stained-glass panels. At the sound of their voices in the entrance hall, Michelle emerged from the sitting-room, glass in hand.

She was taller than her sister, an elegant brunette, as dark as Anne was fair. Wearing a stylish but simple honey-coloured dress split to the thigh, and with a triple row of choker pearls about her throat, she looked as striking as any fashion model.

'Hi, darlings,' she said in a languid fashion. 'I've only been in minutes myself. Sorry I couldn't make the concert, Daddy. How was it?' She pecked her father fleetingly on the cheek while glancing in Anne's direction.

'Superb! You missed a treat,' said Anne, 'and I've had such an enormous meal I shan't need to eat again for a week. How was your evening?'

Michelle raised a weary hand to push back her dark curly fringe. 'Yawn, yawn! I got paired with this guy from one of the advertising film agencies. He was convinced he was on the road to stardom. He also seemed to think *I* might be up for grabs, the creep.' She raised her neat dark eyebrows eloquently. 'Women will never be equal while men see sexual overtones if you're so much as civil to them.'

Her father gave a one-sided smile as they all drifted into the sitting-room. 'One of your disdainful looks would stop a man at fifty paces, my dear! I'm sure you were quite capable of putting him straight.'

'One of my disdainful looks?' His elder daughter laughed. 'Gosh, I must guard against that, mustn't I? It's not easy when you're supposed to be fostering goodwill, et cetera. Luckily we were a party of six, so I feigned a migraine in the end and excused myself.' She perched on the arm of a deep-cushioned chair and took a sip from her glass.

'And now I think I have got a migraine coming! Be sure your sins will find you out, as Nanny would have told me.'

Anne kicked off her high-heeled black patent sandals and tucked her feet up under her on the sofa. 'What's that you're drinking, Mich? The hair of the dog doesn't really help a hangover.'

Her sister made a face at her. 'Pipe down, Nursie! It's not booze, it's health salts—only I have to wait till the fizz goes off—the bubbles give me a headache.'

Their father poured himself a small whisky. 'A few early nights is what you need, my dear, and some healthy exercise to get some fresh air into your lungs. Have some tennis tomorrow, the pair of you. Well, girls, I'm for bed. I'll be away fairly early in the morning. Don't bother to get up.' He said goodnight and left them.

His daughters stayed talking for a while longer. They had not seen each other for some time. Michelle had been on location in Jersey gathering material for a programme on the Nazi occupation of the island, and it had left a deep impression on her, talking to the elderly people who remembered those times.

'A depressing sort of subject,' she sighed, 'but a lot of local heroism. I'm glad I wasn't alive in those days. Anyway, that job's in the can now, thank goodness. What's new on your horizon?'

Anne considered. 'Nothing spectacular.'

'How did you feel, seeing Jon again tonight?'

'No problems . . . why?'

'Oh, come on,' Michelle laughed, 'you were dotty about him once, weren't you?'

'Oh dear,' Anne returned, 'I thought that was a dark secret between me and my conscience. Water under the bridge now, thank goodness. All I feel for him is a certain amount of gratitude that it pushed me into nursing. I really love it, Mich.'

'Still . . . with all this militancy boiling up? What about strike action . . . would you?'

Anne sighed, 'I don't know. I wouldn't want to, but then I'm not as hard up as some of the girls.'

Michelle finished her health salts and put the glass on the Sheraton side table before stretching out on the carpet with a cushion behind her head. 'There's talk of doing a chat show on the state of the Health Service. Do you know of a really dishy doc with ideas of his own who'd agree to join in a question and answer panel?'

'What about an ad in the medical journals?' suggested Anne. 'Or some of your bosses will be bound to have their own top-notch experts. I expect there are dozens of people who'd be only too pleased to air their views.'

'Yes, but what we need is someone with charisma who can also talk sense to the man in the street. You know, the kind of person who gives you faith in the profession.'

'Mmm, it's the things that go wrong which get most publicity these days. Everyday run-of-the-mill good doctoring isn't so newsworthy. But there's a lot of it about.' Anne paused in the act of taking off her gold earrings and a slow smile lifted her thoughtful expression. 'I know a chap who *might* fit the bill, if you could get him to agree, but he may not be the publicity-seeking type.'

Michelle sat up and hugged her knees with interest. 'Who is he?'

'His name's Grant Ryder. He's a neurosurgeon, just back after a year in New York. So he might have one or two interesting comparisons to make about the way things work over here and over there.'

'I like it! Is he young, old? Is he photogenic?'

'Thirtyish. Would tall, dark and handsome suit you, coupled with the most delicious, unaffected dark brown voice?'

'Seems tailor-made for the part.' Michelle yawned and stretched and rubbed the back of her neck. 'When can you introduce me?'

'Oh no! Leave me out of it,' Anne laughed, shaking her head. 'I've hardly spoken to the man. Write to him. Tell him he operated on a friend of your father, which was how you heard about him.'

Anne proceeded to tell her sister about Alistair Carle and his cerebral aneurysm. 'Odd, wasn't it, that Daddy and Jon should both know him. I wasn't aware of that at the time, though.'

'Well, this guy Ryder sounds a possibility,' her sister agreed. She rubbed the back of her neck again. 'My headache is going to get worse, I know. I'll have to take a Valium. Don't think I'll be playing much tennis tomorrow.'

Coming to kneel behind her, Anne began

massaging her sister's shoulders. 'I hope you're not getting hooked on tranquillisers. Where do you get them from?'

'My GP, of course. Ooh, that's lovely, Annie! You should have been a masseuse. I could put up with this for hours.'

'It's probably muscle tension. You ought to learn how to relax . . . join a Yoga class or something.' After massaging for a further five minutes while her sister purred contentedly, Anne said, 'Right, that's your lot, wench. My fingers are giving out. Come on, let's turn in.'

Although it was after two a.m. when the girls went up to their rooms, once in bed Anne couldn't settle to sleep. She picked up the latest copy of *Country Life* and browsed through the pages. The advertisements for palatial country homes sent her thoughts soaring back, recalling idyllic school holidays at their old home in Lamberhurst. That was before childish innocence and wonder were lost in the harsh realism of the world outside.

If their mother had been alive today they would probably have been spending this weekend in the country. But their father had sold Greenacres six months after their mother's fatal riding accident. He now made his home in Kensington, quite content to divide his time between there and his office and his club. Should he need a partner for any social occasion he called upon one of his daughters. Michelle, now divorced, was once more established in a flat of her own, and so the three of them led independent lives.

Anne sighed wistfully, closed the book, put out the light and lay down, thinking about the unpredictable. She brooded on the waste of her mother's life cut short, and she recalled patients whom no amount of care and expertise had been able to save. She hoped Alistair Carle was going to make it. She crossed her fingers for him, which made her think of Grant Ryder's cryptic comment, and she couldn't help smiling. He little knew that wheels had been set in motion which might mean Michelle bursting into his life!

Once Michelle had made up her mind about something she was a lady hard to resist. Not that Anne could imagine Grant Ryder being talked into doing anything he didn't want to do. Then again, she didn't really *know* him as a man, only as a surgeon. One thing, however, she had discovered during their brief meeting. He was not above noticing a humble runner in the operating-room and including her in his tutorial, which was a mark in his favour.

She was looking forward to starting her Neuro course, if only to be able to listen to that fascinating, seductive, mellifluous voice. It somehow managed to be both soothing and exciting. A heady cocktail, and one which should go down well with the public, if Michelle could persuade him to join her TV programme.

CHAPTER TWO

IT WAS nearly eleven the following morning before Anne felt disposed to leave her bed and get the day started. With their father's housekeeper off at weekends, the rest of the house was silent. Trailing down to the kitchen in her dressing-gown, Anne made coffee and took some up to her sister.

'Wakey, wakey!' she called cheerfully, setting the bone china mugs down on the bedside table. She crossed to the window and drew back the rich rose-patterned curtains. Sunlight sparked rainbows from the bevel-edged mirror on the dressing-table. 'Gorgeous morning, Mich—what's left of it,' she said, perching herself on the end of the bed with her drink. 'Come on, stir your lazy bones!'

Michelle yawned and stretched her elegant limbs between the pale pink sheets. 'I've been awake for hours, actually,' she admitted. 'I heard Daddy go, but I couldn't be bothered to move. Thought you'd get around to producing coffee sooner or later.'

Anne sighed good-naturedly. 'If I waited for you to make it we'd be here till tomorrow. How's your head?'

Michelle smoothed back her dark silky hair. 'Oh, better, I think. But I don't feel like being energetic, so don't ask me to play tennis, *please*.' Rousing herself sufficiently to reach for her coffee, she went on, 'I've got a frantically busy day tomorrow. I

27

have to be in Manchester for a meeting by ten a.m., for heaven's sake.'

'Well, I can't say I feel hyperactive either. I wouldn't mind spoiling myself today. Why don't we go to a health club and have a jacuzzi or a sauna and whatever?'

Her sister's face brightened. 'Oh, brilliant! There's the Sanctuary in Covent Garden. The thought of those fluffy white robes and all that cool hanging greenery has got me recycled already. Let's go!'

Some five hours later, after swimming and relaxing and being generally self-indulgent amid the delightful plant-decked, superbly appointed luxury club, the girls emerged refreshed and light of heart.

Michelle set her sunglasses across the top of her hair. 'That was really great—we should do it more often.'

Anne agreed. 'Mmm, bliss, wasn't it? Makes you feel brand new.' She gathered her blonde locks together and clipped them at the back of her head with a tortoiseshell slide.

At six o'clock that Sunday evening the streets around the historic old London market were still thronging with summer visitors. With nothing to hurry them the sisters idled along in carefree fashion, pausing often to glance in the fascinating small shops which bordered the cobbled square.

Always interested in people, Anne found her attention caught by a well-dressed, stocky sightseer. American, she judged, by the style of his hip-hugging blue check trousers and the trim of his sandy hair. He was busy focusing his camera on the colonnaded terraces of the high-vaulted Market Hall. His picture-taking finished, the man joined a friend and they started to stroll in the girls' direction.

Suddenly recognising his companion, Anne caught her breath. 'Oh, no!' she muttered, her pulse quickening. Hastily she turned away to join her sister, studying clothes in a trendy boutique. 'Mich,' she murmured, 'don't look now, but that's him.'

'Which him?' Michelle asked absently, her mind more on fashion.

'There are two fellows coming this way . . .' Anne inclined her head slightly. 'The tall dark one in the jeans . . . that's Grant Ryder, the doctor I was telling you about.'

'*Really?*' Michelle was at once all attention. She stole a look. 'Terrific, Annie. What a heaven-sent opportunity! You can introduce me, can't you?'

'*No!*' Anne yelped. 'I can't! I hardly know him. I was practically anonymous in theatre gear the only time we met. Besides, he's with someone . . .'

At that moment Michelle's eager expression changed to one of lively enquiry as her gaze went over her sister's shoulder.

'Excuse me if I'm mistaken,' began a deep, distinctive voice behind Anne. She spun around, and the speaker went on, 'You *are* Nurse Crossed-fingers, aren't you?'

Her green eyes widening in pretended surprise,

she laughed. 'Hi! Yes, that's me.'

Grant Ryder's own eyes sparkled mischievously. 'You'll be glad to hear that your bonus seems to be working for the patient,' he murmured. 'May I introduce Dr Brad Stevens? I'm afraid I don't know your real name.'

'Anne Westlake,' she said. It surprised her to find her voice sounding quite normal when in fact she felt oddly breathless. 'This is my sister Michelle,' she added, inwardly regretting that the subject of TV programmes had ever been discussed between them and willing Michelle not to mention it.

'Hello! How nice to meet you,' her sister returned, including both men in her winning smile.

'Two lovely ladies from one family!' declared Brad Stevens gallantly. 'You guys are spoiled for choice over here, Grant.'

Ryder gave a tolerant grin. 'Excuse my friend . . . English girls have knocked him for six, it seems. He's over here from the States to see how we do things in the NHS.'

'What was all that about Nurse Crossed-fingers?' asked Michelle, laughing up at him.

A half-smile played around his shapely lips. 'Just a little joke between us. Are you a nurse too?'

'Heaven forbid! We none of us thought Anne would stick it. But now I know why she has,' Michelle returned with an arch grin.

Anne rolled her eyes and sighed. She could cheerfully have throttled her sister. 'Ignore her,' she said. 'Michelle was always blessed with an over-active imagination.'

The American chuckled. 'And where should we be without imagination?'

Grant Ryder changed the subject, his blue eyes searching Anne's. 'Did you enjoy the concert last night?'

Surprise made her frown. 'How did you know . . .?' she began, wondering if she imagined that edge of disapproval in his tone.

'We were there too, honey,' Brad Stevens drawled. 'That's a darned fine set-up you have at the Barbican.'

'Yes, super, isn't it?' Michelle bubbled. 'Sadly, I had to miss out last night. Had to *work!* You're not the only people plagued with unsocial hours, you know.'

'Why, what do you do?' Grant Ryder enquired.

'I'm with a television company.' Delving into her shoulder-bag, Michelle found a business card. 'If you'd like to bring your friend to any of our shows, or to see around the studios, do call me.'

Anne held her breath while Grant Ryder glanced at the card, one dark eyebrow lifting slightly.

'Thank you,' he said, slipping the card into his hip pocket. 'The problem is going to be fitting everything in.'

'I know—it must be,' agreed Michelle, and she let the matter drop.

Relieved though she was, Anne had to admire her sister's strategy. The seed was sown and could conveniently be left to lie fallow for the time being.

Brad Stevens began fiddling with the setting of

his camera. 'May I take your picture, girls? One for my memoirs, if you don't mind? Grant, old buddy, stick yourself between 'em.'

Grant Ryder obligingly took up his position behind them and was duly photographed. Then, at the American's request, the men changed places and Brad Stevens was snapped with his arms around the sisters.

'Great! That'll get the guys green-eyed back home. Look, why don't we all go some place for a drink?'

Grant Ryder checked his wristwatch. 'Sorry, Brad, but we can't really spare the time. Professor Drapper is expecting us at seven-thirty, and we have to change . . .'

Anne had the impression that in any case the surgeon was none too keen to prolong the encounter. 'Oh, we mustn't hold you up.' She turned a pleasant smile on the American. 'Lovely to meet you. Perhaps we'll bump into each other around the hospital some time.'

'Amen to that,' Brad Stevens returned, 'I shall insist Grant makes it happen.'

They parted company and the sisters walked on, intent on finding a place to eat.

'For goodness sake, Annie,' Michelle protested. 'you could have been a bit more forthcoming, couldn't you? You didn't have to leave it all to me.'

Anne shrugged. 'Well, you seemed to be managing all right. I was just hoping you wouldn't mention that wretched programme. Anyway, Mr Ryder obviously didn't want to socialise. It's all very well for you, Mich,' she blurted out, 'but sometimes you do embarrass me. I'm going to have to work with that man, and there's still a lot of class barriers in hospitals, you know. I'm only a staff nurse.'

'*Only!*' Michelle hooted with derision. 'Don't be so modest. Hospitals couldn't function without nurses, so it's time they got their priorities right. You could walk out tomorrow if you wanted to. And if those two saw you with Daddy last night they must have tumbled that socially you move in acceptable circles.'

'Unless they thought he was my *sugar* daddy,' Anne conjectured, which made both girls collapse with laughter.

'What's Ryder's history, do you know?' Michelle asked later, when they were served with a succulent pizza in a little Italian café.

'Not the faintest—except that he's lately been in New York and that he's going to be Prof Drapper's right-hand man. On second thoughts, that's someone who might be better for your programme,' said Anne. 'He's a pet.'

'How old?'

'Sixty-fiveish, I should think. Looks sort of Pickwickian.'

'Uh-uh!' Michelle shook her head and took a long drink of Chablis. 'It's the up-and-coming go-getters we're after. TV is all about the beautiful people, or hadn't you noticed?'

Anne smiled. 'I wouldn't agree entirely. I'd have thought personality is what counts. Still, you know what you're looking for, and if you can persuade the gorgeous Grant, good luck to you. But I wouldn't bet on it.'

Coming back to the flat which she shared with Mandy was like coming back to sanity after a day spent in Michelle's effervescent company. Mandy represented stability and normality. She was the youngest daughter of a Devonshire Methodist minister. Her mother had died from a heart problem shortly after Anne's own mother met her untimely death and the common bond of sympathy had drawn them close.

Hearing Anne's arrival, Mandy came from her room fastening the white collar on her clean saxe-blue uniform. 'Hiya, pal,' she breezed. 'Had a good day . . . what did you do?'

'Spent it with Mich. We were both feeling a bit jaded, so we treated ourselves . . .'

On hearing the details, Mandy whistled. 'Bet that cost a bomb! Still, you can't take it with you, as they say. Be a pal and make me a cuppa, will you? I'm running a bit late.'

'Sure.' Anne went through to their tiny kitchenette, made tea for them both and carried it through to Mandy's room, where she flopped on the bed, watching her flatmate finish dressing.

'My last night on, thank goodness,' Mandy rejoiced, fishing her black lace-up shoes from under the chair, 'then you'll have the place to yourself for a fortnight.'

'. . . and no one to moan to if my new course

turns out to be ghastly,' Anne said. 'Better leave me
your home number, I'll probably be on the phone
every night!'

Mandy laughed, taking a gulp of tea in between
slipping pencil torch, pen and scissors into her
pocket. 'And *that* would cost you some. Can't
think why you chose Neuro anyway, when you
could have done A & E with me.'

'We-ell, I prefer my patients with their bits and
pieces nicely tidied up, not spread all over the
trolley. Anyway, I've always liked Prof Drapper,
and Bob Ramsgate's a good sort, isn't he?
Honestly, I think it's going to be really fascinating.
The only unknown quantity at the moment is the
new reg, Grant Ryder. Have you met him yet?'
Anne asked.

'Yep. We had to call him in for a skull fracture
last night, as a matter of fact.' Mandy dashed a
brush through her spiky brown hair and stuffed her
navy cardigan into her holdall. 'Wow, that voice!'
She chuckled. 'Like being stroked in all the right
places. Well, I'm off. See you in the morning.
'Bye!' She collected her bicycle from the narrow
hallway and was gone, leaving Anne to her
thoughts about where her chosen course would
lead her.

In a comfortable sitting-room at the School of
Nursing chairs had been placed in a half-circle
around a table. There were eight nurses gathered to
start the Neurological course that Monday
morning. Three of them were girls Anne knew,

having trained with them at St Martin's, but the others were from outside hospitals. They all stood chatting together, getting acquainted while waiting for their tutor to appear.

Tutor Mrs Shore breezed in promptly at nine o'clock, clutching an armful of pink ring-bound folders, a plumply comfortable woman in her late forties.

'Good morning, everyone. Do sit yourselves down,' she said in a sociable manner. Dumping the folders on the table, she propped herself against it and waited until the scraping of chairs ceased and they were all settled.

Anne found a seat next to Hazel, a tall, slim girl from St Mary's with whom she had been talking, and smiled back expectantly at Mrs Shore's pleasant round face. They were no strangers, having come into contact often during Anne's student days.

When she had their attention the tutor began, 'This morning is going to be an informal session so that we can all get to know each other. To begin with, I thought you might like to hear why you were chosen for the course from among the many who applied. Our consultant, Professor Drapper, aims to have a nice blend of personalities in his wards. It was considered that you all displayed the desired traits of friendliness, self-confidence and professionalism. We felt that you would make a good team.'

She glanced all round, smiling briefly. 'The Professor also likes to encourage social activities among the staff. He thinks it's good for morale, and I'm sure he's right. We hope you'll be prepared to join in whatever can be arranged. Now, if you'd like to introduce yourselves to each other, then we'll discuss the programme.'

There was a short pause and smiles all round before Anne spoke up. 'Actually we covered that before you came in, Mrs Shore.'

Their tutor nodded approvingly. 'Fine—I should have been disappointed if you hadn't.' She began distributing the folders, one to each of them. 'Well, here is your syllabus for the next six months. Have a browse through it. You'll see the first week is given over to lectures and films and visits, before we let you loose in the department. Then there'll be further study days throughout the course. It's a good programme. It should qualify you for a sister's post in the speciality in due course.'

There was a rustling of pages while the tutor gave the class time to look at the syllabus.

After questions and comments, she went on, 'Naturally the theoretical side of things is important, but the best way to learn a new job is by practice. There's nothing to beat experience at the bedside, under the right guidance. You are going to have a mass of technology to deal with, as those of you know who have spent time in ITU. Some of your patients' lives may depend upon it. But try to remember that it's you, as nurses, who are their human lifeline. However marvellous our machines, only people can supply that kindly word and soothing touch.'

Hazel cast a mock-comic glance at Anne and said, in an audible aside, 'Bother! Forgot to pack my halo!'

Mrs Shore joined in the general laughter. 'OK, we'll break for coffee now,' she said. 'Hazel, you can spread your sprouting wings and get it. Perhaps you'll show her where the kitchen is, Anne. And bring an extra cup for Mr Ryder. He should be here any time now to give you your introductory talk on the aims and philosophy of the course. Professor Drapper usually does it, but he's not available today.'

Leaving the others happily exchanging views, Anne took Hazel along to the kitchen.

'I'll be glad when this first week is over,' sighed Hazel, placing cups and saucers on the trolley. 'I much prefer getting on with the job to talking about it. Do you know this fellow Ryder—what's he like?'

'*Very* dishy!' Anne pronounced with a broad grin.

'Oh! And an outsized ego to match, no doubt.' Hazel groaned and pushed her straight brown fringe back from her forehead. 'I prefer the homely sort myself. They get less spoiled.'

'Actually he hasn't been around here long, so the grapevine hasn't got working yet. We shall have to see.'

Anne busied herself putting biscuits on a plate while they waited for the kettle to boil. She felt oddly tense, her enthusiasm for the course tinged with a certain amount of apprehension. Which was only natural, she told herself, when you were on the threshold of a new experience. It was the unpredictable, as Grant Ryder had so aptly put it in theatre the other day; certainly it had nothing to do with the fact that *he* was now to be part of her working life.

'Well, at least Mrs Shore's game for a laugh,' Hazel approved. 'I did wonder, when she started on about soothing the fevered brow and all that. I mean, if you need *telling*, what brought you to nursing in the first place? She'll be dishing us out with lamps next, *à la* Nightingale, I thought.'

Anne chuckled. She could see why this girl had been chosen for the course. A sense of the ridiculous always helped to lighten the load. 'Come on,' she urged, pouring milk into a jug, 'better get this lot in there or she'll think we've chickened out.'

'OK, you go ahead . . . I must just go to the loo.' Hazel dashed off towards the cloakroom in the corridor.

Pushing the tea-trolley, Anne came to the door of the sitting-room at the same time as Grant Ryder. He was dressed today in a formal grey lounge suit with crisp blue shirt and college tie, every inch the elegant professional.

'Hello!' he exclaimed, his brow puckering in that quizzical fashion she was beginning to find bone-melting. 'Not *you* again! You seem to be dogging my footsteps lately.'

'Or one could say you seem to be dogging mine,' she replied smoothly.

'Are you taking this course?' he asked in some surprise. 'I thought you were theatre staff.'

'Oh, I was just filling in time there until this started.'

He stood with his hand on the door, controlling a smile. 'I warn you, we expect a great deal more of our nurses than crossed fingers.'

Giving an exaggerated sigh, Anne returned, 'Oh, do shut up! You're not going to let me forget I said that, are you?'

He seemed, for the moment, at a loss for words, and she smiled at him artlessly. It was probably a novel experience for him, these days, being told to shut up. And by a nurse, at that!

There was a hint of amusement in his tone when he deigned to reply, 'Probably not. It depends how you behave yourself.'

She was saved from thinking of a rejoinder to that by Hazel's timely arrival, and he pushed open the door to let them both through.

During the coffee-break Grant Ryder insisted on meeting all the nurses, learning their names and something of their previous histories, which at once endeared him to the class. Hazel, after an animated conversation with him, was quite won over.

'I take back all I said,' she murmured afterwards to Anne. 'He'll do.' She looked a little puzzled. 'Why didn't you talk to him? He's very approachable.'

'I'd spoken to him earlier,' Anne pointed out. But she couldn't help feeling slightly miffed that he'd given her barely a passing glance after their first encounter. Well, if he wanted to stand on his dignity, so be it.

The business of the day resumed with Mrs Shore calling for their attention so that the neurosurgeon could deliver his talk.

Propping himself against the table, hands thrust into his trouser pockets, Grant Ryder surveyed the attentive faces before him. All intelligent young women—short, tall, thin, plump—and Nurse Crossed-fingers—begging her pardon—too pretty by half and confident with it.

'In truth,' he said, a modest smile animating his dark good looks, 'I'd rather be dealing with a difficult spinal tumour any day than giving lectures, but, since the Professor has lumbered me, here goes.'

For all his professed reluctance, he was a fluent speaker with a persuasive manner, and within the first five minutes he had his audience in his grasp. He talked to them for a good hour, not concealing the fact that there would be the heartaches as well as the hoorays. He made them think; he made them laugh. He concluded by saying, 'I hope I have convinced you that neurology is an exciting and rewarding branch of medicine—not to be confused with psychiatry—and not in the least depressing. We do see many happy results. Any questions?'

His keen blue eyes roved over the nurses and came to rest on Anne, who had been as transfixed as the others. She half smiled at him, whereupon he directed his gaze elsewhere, not wishing to be seduced by a pair of soft green eyes and a cloud of ash-blonde hair. 'Oh, so you think you know everything already, do you?' he observed, with a satirical twist of his well-defined lips.

One or two people laughed before Anne spoke up. 'There is a limit to how much one can take in at a sitting, Mr Ryder.'

The surgeon's steady gaze returned to this glib young woman. She spoke politely, but with a touch of mischief in her manner. The girl had the poise and self-assurance that came from good breeding. He had recognised the same thing in her sister. They had a style about them, an effortless charm. He guessed they had never wanted for anything in their lives.

'Exactly,' he returned, surprising himself by almost snapping, 'but don't fall into the trap of believing blindly everything you're told. Scepticism is essential in good medicine. Question everything. Even things in print are not necessarily true—they may be just one person's viewpoint. Temper everything with your own good sense. All right?' He shot her a straight glance. She nodded but said nothing more.

'Fine!' He glanced at his watch, then rewarded the rest of the class with his heartwarming smile. 'We'll leave it there for now. I'll let you get some lunch.'

'That'll teach you to open your big mouth,' quipped Hazel, her eyes on the dynamic surgeon, who had stayed for a private word with their tutor before leaving.

Anne nibbled her thumbnail, inwardly piqued. 'I'm blowed if I was going to sit there and be patronised,' she said.

'Oh, come on,' the other girl laughed, 'he was only trying to be funny.'

'At our expense,' Anne pointed out. 'Still, maybe he's more used to dealing with cocky medical students than qualified nurses.'

'Well, don't let it bug you. Come and find some food—my stomach's calling *mayday!*'

They followed the rest of the group over to the canteen, where the debate on the morning's lecture continued until the start of their afternoon programme.

Everyone was in high spirits, agreeing on the excellence of Grant Ryder's encouraging introductory talk. Everyone also agreed that they thought the surgeon was stunning.

'A real heartjerker,' sighed Sara Downs, a girl from the Midlands. 'Wonder if he's married?'

'No, he isn't,' Anne told them, having gathered as much while she was in theatre.

A lot of laughing speculation followed, but Anne was quiet. Truth to tell, she actually felt hurt. After all, there had been no reason for him to be so brusque with her in the class. All she had done was to make a perfectly innocent comment because nobody else seemed to have anything to say. Maybe nurses should be seen and not heard in his book. At least, that was what it seemed like where she was concerned. For some peculiar reason he seemed to delight in picking her up on whatever she said. Very well, in future she would say as little as possible!

CHAPTER THREE

BY FRIDAY of that first week the class had covered a great deal of ground. There had been talks from the anaesthetist and radiologist, films on a variety of procedures and a visit to a spinal injuries unit. Their final session was a tour of the four wards on the neurological floor, meeting other members of staff and being briefed on the sophisticated equipment in the high-dependency rooms.

'Well now,' said Mrs Shore when they were assembled in her office to be told where they would be working the following week, 'as I told you, Professor Drapper likes to encourage the social side of the unit, so he wishes to meet you all. He's arranged a tea-party in the residents' dining-room. Will you be over there at five o'clock, please?'

Uniforms had not been called for during their study week and the nurses on the course were in casual clothes. Everyone made for the staff-room and a quick freshen up.

''Wish we'd known about this,' groaned Hazel, rubbing a spot of orange juice from her striped cotton T-shirt. 'I'd have put on something decent.'

'You look OK,' said Anne, adjusting the belt around her own pink flying suit. 'Anyway, we're all in the same boat, and it probably won't be that sort of party. Just an informal welcome over a cup of tea, I expect.'

Along with the rest of the group they sauntered across the main square which separated the hospital from the medical college and the residents' quarters.

'I wonder who'll be there?' Hazel pondered. 'Do you think Ryder will be?'

'It depends on whether he's free, I suppose.' Anne couldn't help being amused at the interest in the other girl's voice. Much to most people's disappointment, they'd had no more contact with the senior registrar since his initial talk. 'Don't tell me you fancy him?' she teased.

Hazel grinned and flaunted the diamond ring on her left hand. 'I'm engaged, but I can look, can't I? And you must admit, he *is* fanciable.'

Anne was admitting nothing. The forthright doctor had been much on her mind. She was reluctant to tangle with him again and she resolved to steer clear of him should he be at the party.

For heaven's sake, he's just a man, she told herself, swallowing against a ridiculous tightness in her throat. So he was a clever surgeon, but that didn't give him the right to patronise the nursing staff. Nevertheless, she approached the residents' dining-room in a mild state of panic, letting Hazel's chatter pass over her head.

When the girls entered the dining-room the party was already off to a good start. Among those present were a number of nurses and sisters who had been on early duty on the neuro wards, and housemen and staff from associated departments. Everyone seemed on friendly terms, regardless of status.

On a long central table an inviting buffet was laid out, while at a side table the genial, silver-haired Professor Drapper was actually dispensing tea from a large teapot. Alongside him, Mrs Shore assisted by pouring milk into cups.

'Now I've seen everything!' murmured Hazel, wide-eyed. 'He really does mean this one big happy family stuff.'

Anne was more concerned with checking out the rest of the company. She didn't know whether to be glad or sorry that the disturbing Grant Ryder was nowhere in sight. Catching her eye, Mrs Shore smiled and beckoned them over.

'Come on, Hazel,' said Anne, 'we're being summoned to report.'

Putting down his teapot, the Professor shook their hands warmly, eyeing the girls over his half-glasses. 'Ah, yes . . . I remember you now. Anne, you trained here, didn't you? And Hazel, this is new ground for you.' He beamed at them both. 'Looking forward to your time with us, I hope? Never be afraid to ask questions, my dears. You'll soon get into the swing of things. Well, off you go and get circulating.'

The courtesies over, they helped themselves to food and fell into conversation with Mary Glynn, a small chestnut-haired Welsh woman, one of the sisters on Fleming, the male neurosurgical ward. Both Anne and Hazel were due to start work there the following week.

'. . . and glad we are to have you,' Mary enthused.

'Staffing is a headache when you get a number of patients needing to be specialled.' Laughing, she went on, 'You're going to have to get used to holding one-sided conversations now and then, girls! Well, you must excuse me, I have to go. There's an open evening at my son's school and I'll be in the doghouse if I'm late. See you on Monday. Goodbye.'

Noting the sister's ingratiating manner as she took her leave of the Professor, Anne said doubtfully, 'She seems OK, doesn't she?'

Hazel pursed her lips. 'Goes on a bit, but perhaps she was only trying to be matey. Well, since we're here to circulate, I suppose we ought. I'm going to talk to that fellow from X-Ray. See you later,' and she wandered off.

Spotting the lanky figure of Bob Ramsgate on his own at the far end of the buffet table, Anne made tracks to talk to him.

'Hi, Bob,' she said brightly. 'I haven't seen you since we did Mr Carle's aneurysm.'

A slow smile lightened his rather sober features. 'Annie, hello! Have a chicken vol-au-vent? They're good.' He passed her the plate and they stood together eating, chatting agreeably.

'Mr Carle's op . . . that takes me back a bit,' reflected Bob. 'There've been a few more since then.'

'Actually, it's only a week ago. How is he?'

'Super. His wife wanted him transferred to the London Clinic, but he said he couldn't be better cared for than where he is and refused to move.'

'House point for Marty's!' Anne crowed.

Bob pushed his gold-rimmed glasses further up on his long nose, regarding her with mild interest. 'One of his visitors was asking about you today.'

'About me?' She frowned. 'Who was that?'

'Don't know his name . . . he didn't say. I believe he also knows your father. Not short of cash, by the look of him.'

'Oh, probably a business connection,' she returned carelessly, despairing at how difficult it was to keep one's private life private. 'My father does know Mr Carle slightly. I expect they have friends in common.' She supposed the visitor might have been Jonathan Locke and was glad she hadn't been on the ward at the time. 'How are you finding your new boss?' she asked.

'Ryder? Great, so far. Not that I've had much to do with him yet, apart from work, that is.' The SHO popped a last titbit into his mouth and wiped his fingers on a paper napkin. 'He's been tied up with this American chap. They were both supposed to be coming . . .' Bob looked beyond her towards the nearby door as it was pushed open. 'Ah, this may be them.'

Quickly Anne glanced around, prepared to move on, but she saw only Georges Alain, the dark-bearded anaesthetist, accompanied by the American. And so she stayed put and laughed as Brad Stevens struck a pose of delighted surprise on seeing her.

'There you are!' he exclaimed. 'I was beginning to think you were a figment of my imagination.

Where've you been hiding your delightful self?'

'Oh, you've met before, 'ave you?' Georges's dark eyes twinkled and he wagged a forefinger at the visitor. 'Now, now, sir. 'ands off our nurses! We can't 'ave you running off with our staff.'

Anne grinned. 'Don't worry, Georges, it would take a lot to persuade me to go to America.'

The anaesthetist put an arm around her shoulders and gave her a hug. 'I am very glad to 'ear it, little one.'

Bradley Stevens was gazing around. 'Grant not here yet? Must have got held up somewhere.'

'That's life!' Anne put in blithely. She stayed chatting with the doctors for a few more minutes before excusing herself to join some of the other nurses.

When the tea-party came to a close one of the girls suggested migrating to the Jolly Friars for a final drink before they parted and duties separated them.

Seated in an alcove in the low-ceilinged oak-panelled pub, the eight nurses swapped news and views of their impressions to date.

'I'm really sorry the week's over,' mourned Sara, the girl from the Midlands.'I enjoyed being back at school again. And London's so enormous, I'm going to feel like a refugee once we've all split up.' She pulled a tragic face.

'For goodness' sake,' Anne laughed, 'we'll see each other around. Where are you living?'

'The nurses' home. There's not a face I know on my floor. *And* somebody nicked my milk out of the fridge yesterday.'

Remembering how lonely she had felt when she'd first come to St Martin's, Anne had a brainwave. 'Anyone free tomorrow night? My flatmate's away, so if you'd all like to come round to the flat I'll rustle up a meal and we can have a hen party. How about it?'

There were cries of approval and offers of help. Finally, with everyone primed on how to find where Anne lived, they parted company in good heart.

As she returned to the hospital to collect her bicycle, Anne's mood was upbeat and carefree. Entering through the wrought-iron gates leading to the square in front of the main entrance, she smiled a 'good evening' to the doorman at the lodge. Light filtered softly through the plane trees. At eight o'clock there were still plenty of people about—visitors, porters, nurses, doctors—all going their separate ways. But there was a tranquillity pervading this shady oasis in the heart of London, a certain magic which made her glad to be part of it.

Having extricated her bicycle from between others chained to some railings, she dropped her shoulder-bag and lecture notes in the basket, hitched herself on to the saddle and rode slowly along the path that led to a side gate out. Preoccupied with plans for the following evening, she almost ran down Grant Ryder, coming from the residents' quarters, before she saw him and wobbled alarmingly.

'Whoa there!' He placed a steadying hand on her handlebars and fixed her with that frowning half-smile which she had found so fascinating. 'Where are you off to with such reckless abandon?'

'Just home,' she said, resting one foot on the ground, her calm smile belying the weakness in her limbs.

Looking up into his strong, ascetic features, pearly teeth faintly visible between his parted lips, Anne was acutely conscious of the dark-lashed eyes assessing her. Face to face with him like this, she sensed a kind of challenge. There was also a subtle magnetism between them, and in a strange way she was convinced that he too felt the emotive undercurrent. She knew he was aware of her as a woman as well as a nurse.

'Oh!' he said, after a moment. 'So it wasn't another romantic assignation which brought that faraway look to your eyes?'

'Another what?' she asked with a puzzled smile.

'Well, you did have an attentive escort at the Barbican the other night.'

Anne laughed. 'Oh, that was my father, and a friend. I'm hardly likely to be dating men twice my age, am I?'

Grant considered the information, his lips twitching. 'It has been known. All right, so where's home? Far to go?'

She met his enquiring gaze levelly. 'About twenty minutes' ride. I share a flat with a girl in Finsbury.'

'I see. I thought it was a long way to be cycling

if you lived with your sister in Hampstead.'

Anne laughed again. 'No, I don't live with Mich. But how did you know she lives in Hampstead? I thought it was her business card she gave you?'

'So she did,' Grant nodded. 'She also made me miss the Professor's tea-party this afternoon,' he added, a touch of annoyance now creeping into his tone.

Anne frowned, her mind going into a spin. How had Michelle managed to arrange an interview at such short notice? 'I didn't know she was seeing you today?'

'I didn't say she had. She telephoned, but if she hadn't kept me talking Dr Arbuthnot wouldn't have collared me to discuss a patient. Which was how I came to miss the bunfight. I wasn't too popular in some quarters.'

Anne despaired of her sister. She couldn't understand what had possessed her to go ringing the doctor at the hospital about a private matter. If it concerned the TV programme, wouldn't a letter have been the right approach to begin with?

'I'm terribly sorry,' she said, 'I had no idea Mich intended to do that. She should have realised you'd be busy.' She shrugged lamely. 'I'm afraid my sister lives in a totally different world from ours.'

Grant stroked his lean jaw reflectively, taking in her rising colour. Her cheeks were as pink as her flying suit, and that little dusting of freckles across her nose looked slightly moist. He'd actually discomfited the cool Miss Crossed-fingers!

'Don't worry about it,' he returned with a great

show of tolerance. 'As a matter of fact I thought it
a generous gesture on her part, wanting to give a
dinner-party for Brad Stevens. Something about
making her contribution to international goodwill.
Anyway, that's what the lady said. I imagined you
would have been in the picture?'

'Good heavens, no.' Anne shook her head. 'I'm
the last person to know anything about my sister's
plans.'

The doctor smiled wryly. 'Oh, like that, is it?
Sibling rivalry?'

She lifted her small chin proudly. 'No, Michelle
and I are the best of pals. Our lives just happen not
to interlock, that's all.'

He twisted her lecture notebook in the bicycle
basket, reading her name on the cover. 'Her
surname's different too. How's that?'

'Michelle's married, or rather, she was.'

'Ah!' Grant raised an understanding eyebrow, as
though this explained a lot. He tinkled her bicycle
bell. 'Well, mind how you go on your boneshaker
or your sister will be holding a wake, not a party.
Goodnight.' He strode on his way back towards the
hospital.

Regretting the day she'd ever been crazy enough
to mention his name to Michelle, Anne pedalled on
towards the flat, her former happy mood in shreds.
She was mad with herself, mad with her sister, and,
most of all, mad with Grant Ryder. That smirk on
his handsome face had been infuriating. And to
think he'd even had her apologising!

She couldn't wait to get home and find out what

her sister was up to. International goodwill? Generous gestures? That was rich! Anne suddenly giggled to herself. Michelle always knew what she was doing. Her generous impulses were hardly ever without ulterior motives, as Grant Ryder would doubtless discover in due course.

As to that disturbingly erotic sensation she'd experienced while they were talking, it was probably just the age-old battle between the sexes. He'd known she was embarrassed and he'd enjoyed it. She gritted her teeth and thought dark thoughts about the superior registrar. One big happy family, were they? Well, *he* was certainly not going out of his way to spread sweetness and light where she was concerned!

On reaching the flat Anne hastened to dial her sister's number. Disappointingly, there was no reply, so she had to curb her impatience for the time being.

Anne's proposed small hen party on Saturday night managed to become quite a different affair by the time it happened. In the supermarket that morning she met Jane and Geoff from the flat upstairs.

'What, no fellers? Hey, come on, Annie, we can't have that,' breezed Geoff. 'Let's do the job properly and have a really mega effort. Jane'll help with the chores, won't you, baby?'

'Do I have any option?' laughed his girlfriend. 'No, honestly, I'd love to help.'

In the end at least twenty people turned up to Anne's get-together. Two of the neuro nurses brought their boyfriends and Anne invited Bob Ramsgate because she felt he could probably do with a break from studying for his FRCS.

'What are we celebrating?' Bob asked, jiving away to a lively tape, more relaxed than she had ever seen him.

'Just life,' grinned Anne, swinging to the music, all problems shelved for the present.

'Good thinking, anyway. Funny how impromptu rave-ups often turn out to be the best.' He cocked an ear. 'Is that your telephone ringing?'

'Yes, it is!' Anne squeezed her way past the dancers to answer it.

'Good gracious, what's all the noise?' asked Michelle. 'You having an orgy there?'

'Just a few friends in,' Anne said, laughing. She clamped her hand over her other ear and raised her voice slightly. 'Sorry, what was that, Mich? Oh, look, I can hardly hear myself speak at the moment, let alone you. Ring you back in the morning. All right?'

'OK,' her sister yelled, 'just wanted to warn you to keep next Friday evening free. 'Bye!' and she rang off.

Wondering what to make of that, Anne ran a frustrated hand through her hair. She imagined it must be about the dinner-party Grant Ryder had mentioned. She had been thinking about it, off and on, not knowing if she was included in Michelle's plans and not at all sure that it was a good idea. It was possible, of course, that meeting the surgeon on equal terms in a civilised social setting might help their working relationship. On the other hand it might make things more difficult.

There was little point in worrying about it until it happened. Sighing philosophically, Anne went back to her guests.

Her own party finally ran out of steam around two a.m. She was left with Bob and another fairly mellow houseman, both of whom had decided to crash out on the sofa, and Hazel and Sara who stayed on to help clear up the aftermath.

The three girls surveyed the dirty plates and glasses piled in the small kitchen and wrinkled their noses at each other.

Anne yawned. 'I can't face this lot tonight. Let's leave it. I'll do it tomorrow. There's my flatmate's bed you could share, if you'd like to stay over . . .'

That agreed, they all went to bed.

It was late on Sunday morning before Anne roused the stragglers with mugs of coffee, and well past lunchtime before the last of the guests departed. Then, at last, she was able to satisfy her mounting curiosity by returning Michelle's telephone call.

As she had supposed, her sister had rung to talk about the dinner-party she planned to give for Grant Ryder and the American.

'You certainly don't let the grass grow under your feet,' Anne sighed. 'And all that hooey you gave Grant about international goodwill . . . honestly, Mich, you should be in politics!'

Her sister laughed. 'Well, it's partly true. So he told you I'd rung, did he?'

'He happened to mention it. I don't think he believed I knew nothing about it. And he was a bit put out because you interrupted his timetable.'

'Dear me, how dreadful!' Michelle mocked. 'Anyway, I've spoken to him again since then, and they can both make next Friday, as I'd hoped. There'll be my producer and his PA,' she rattled on, 'and with you, that'll make six of us.'

Anne cut in, 'Hang on a minute, Mich! You don't actually need me, do you? I mean, if you're going to talk shop—and I suppose that's what it's all about—I'd rather not be involved. You could find someone else , couldn't you?'

'Oh, come on, Annie, of course I need you,' Michelle insisted. 'You're my entrée. Anyway, it'll be good for your image. And there'll be no chores to do, because I'm getting Taste Buds to do the catering—they're a local firm. I've used them before, and they're terrific. So all you'll have to do is look decorative and be charming. You will be able to make it, won't you?' her sister wheedled.

'Oh, all right, you've talked me into it,' Anne replied with her usual good humour.

By the time they had finished discussing the details she was beginning to feel as enthusiastic as Michelle about the prospect. Michelle's luxury flat in Hampstead was perfect for an intimate dinner-party. The French windows of her living-room opened on to a patio and a small walled garden, ideal for entertaining on warm summer nights.

Putting down the phone, Anne reminded herself

that one could become too insular, mixing endlessly with the same old hospital crowd. It would be a welcome change meeting people from her sister's totally different world. In any case, she liked Brad Stevens, brash though he was. There would be no harm in showing him a bit of 'international goodwill', as Michelle had put it.

Grant Ryder, however, was something else. Anne had no idea what his reaction would be when he discovered the real purpose of Michelle's generosity. Would he really believe she hadn't been part of the conspiracy? Oh, well, let him think what he liked. She didn't care.

For the moment Anne had more important things to think about, like starting work on Fleming Ward. It was responsible work and the high-tech equipment would demand all her powers of concentration. Glad at last to be getting to grips with the real job, she searched out a clean saxe-blue uniform from among a pile of washing and ironed it ready for the morning.

Before going to bed she decided on a nice long chat with Mandy to bring her up to date with affairs. Far from ringing every night, as Anne had originally threatened, she had had so much going on she'd hardly had time to think about it.

Her call to the Devon manse was answered by the minister, Mandy's father. 'Oh, Annie,' he said, 'she's not here, I'm afraid. She's at the local hospital—trod on a broken bottle in the sea this morning and cut her foot.'

'Oh, dear, I *am* sorry. How bad is it?' Anne asked.

'Well, it was a very deep cut and bled a lot, and of course there was sand it in. They're keeping her overnight. I don't suppose she'll be getting a shoe on for some time, so she won't be back to London for a while. I shall ring St Martin's tomorrow.'

Anne sent her love. 'And tell her I miss her—I do hope she gets on all right.'

'Well, out of every adversity comes a blessing,' the minister declared. 'For my part, I shall enjoy having her home for a little while longer.'

Anne doubted that her flatmate would regard it as a blessing! Poor Mandy! she thought ruefully. You could never tell when fate was going to deal you a joker.

CHAPTER FOUR

ANNE'S alarm woke her at six-thirty the next day. Drawing back her bedroom curtains, she found London shrouded in a persistent grey drizzle. Traffic swished along the wet road, the plane trees dripped from every point of their broad leaves, and pigeons perched in bedraggled fortitude under the eaves of the houses opposite. Not a morning for hiking to the Underground or cycling, she decided, especially when there was a taxi rank around the corner.

'St Martin's, please,' she said, putting down her umbrella and climbing into the first cab available.

'Righto, love.' The middle-aged cabby flicked down his 'For Hire' sign and headed his vehicle in the direction of the hospital. He was a chatty Cockney character who kept up a flow of small talk on their journey. 'Been in there a couple o'times meself,' he said. 'Smashin' place. Couldn't have been treated better if I was royalty.'

'That's nice to hear.' Anne looked at her watch while they sat, inching forward, in a long line of traffic.

'You a nurse, then?'

'Yes. I usually cycle, but I didn't fancy arriving like a drowned rat. I'm on at seven-thirty . . . am I going to make it?'

'Or you'll have the Matron on your back, eh?

61

Not to worry, love. We'll get you there.' The cabby expertly made a swift U-turn, doubled in and out of back streets and finally deposited her at the gates with more than five minutes to spare.

'Thanks, you're a real pal.' She smiled gratefully and held out the fare money.

He waved it away. 'Be my guest, love,' he said, and when she tried to insist he winked broadly. 'Go on, scarper. I only do it for the ones I fancy.'

Laughing, Anne thanked him again and dashed through the rain into the hospital, where she took the lift to the neurological floor. In the now empty staff-room she dumped her belongings, pinned her muslin cap on her hastily tidied blonde hair and hurried along to Fleming Ward, a little breathless, but on time for report. Or rather, she would have been, but for unforeseen circumstances.

Scarcely had she pushed open the swing doors before she was waylaid by a middle-aged man in a dressing-gown who shot from the patients' toilets as though the devil was after him.

'Nurse, quick, there's a bloke in there having a fit,' he said urgently, jerking his thumb.

'Oh!' Anne altered course. 'Tell Sister, will you, please?' she threw over her shoulder on her way to investigate.

She found a youngish, pyjama-clad man on the floor by the wash-basins, his limbs jerking violently. Anne had met with fits and convulsions a number of times during her nursing career, but it was always a rather distressing sight even for the professional. There was little to be done for him at the moment, other than making sure his airway was clear and that he did not hurt himself.

After a couple of minutes his convulsive movements subsided. Then she was able to turn him into the safe, semi-prone position, which she was engaged in doing when Sister Mary hurried in, accompanied by her junior charge nurse, Don Hyde.

'Oh, it's Terry Walters!' Mary exclaimed, dropping to her knees beside the patient. 'What happened . . . did you see him fall?' she asked, looking across at Anne.

'No, Sister, he was in the clonic stage when I arrived.' Anne paused. 'Is he a known epileptic?'

'No, he's here for observation. Concussion after falling off a ladder. He should be having an EEG today.' Lifting each eyelid of the now quietly comatose patient, the sister shone her pencil torch to test his pupil reactions. 'Hell, no responses, he's out cold.' Getting to her feet, she refixed a white hair-clip in the frilled cap on her reddish hair. 'Don, get someone to help you put him to bed and clean him up. I'll have to bleep the SHO. And I haven't taken report yet, and there's poor Mr Smith's wife to break the news to, and it's Drapper's round this morning. This is *all* we need!' She sighed heavily. 'Anne, you wait here until Don comes back, then come along to the office to catch up on report.'

The charge nurse, an amiable West Indian, followed the sister out, returning with a trolley and an orderly. 'Looks like being one of those days!' he said cheerfully. 'And there's a rumour the domestics are threatening to strike. Great life, isn't it?'

Anne smiled wryly, helping to place the unfortunate Terry Walters safely on the trolley. 'Oh, terrific. This must have been staged especially for my benefit,' she joked. 'What happened to Mr Smith?'

'He had a haematemesis this morning—his gastric ulcer blew up. All he came in for was removal of a benign cyst, poor bloke. Anyway, nothing for us to worry about now. He's been transferred to a medical ward. Right, better get this boyo tidied up,' and he wheeled their patient away.

By the end of that day it seemed to Anne that she had landed in the middle of a cross between high drama and farce. Her first nursing task, after helping to serve breakfasts to those patients who qualified, was to assist with the care of an unconscious patient on a ventilator.

The solidly built young man in his thirties was in a single room where a complex array of machines hummed and flickered, maintaining his frail hold on life. Many get-well cards were plastered over the wall opposite his bed, together with a notice which said 'Our patient may not be able to talk, but he may be able to hear!'

His special nurse—Jenny—smiled a welcome to Anne and informed her totally unresponsive charge, 'Michael, Anne is here to help me this morning. We're going to wash you now, and make your bed.'

'Good morning, Michael,' Anne returned,

following the other girl's example. They lowered the cot sides and began to turn back the bedclothes.

'Gosh, what a rotten morning . . . it's still raining cats and dogs out there. Good job it's not St Swithin's Day yet . . .' Jenny went on.

'No, that's next week.' Anne placed the folded quilt over a chair.

All through the processes of care the girls chatted, including the apparently unhearing patient in their conversation. As Anne already knew, there was much careful nursing needed with comatose patients. Their position must be changed frequently, limbs moved to avoid deformity, fluid intake and output measured, levels of consciousness watched for, and tracheal secretions cleared.

'How long has Michael been here?' she asked, straightening her side of the sheet while Jenny held the young man to her.

'Four weeks now,' said Jenny. 'Depressed skull fracture. Came off his motorbike, didn't you, love?' Rearranging her patient's head on the flat pillow, she lovingly combed the front of his lank brown hair.

The tenderness in the other girl's voice brought a tightness to Anne's throat. 'Anything more I can do?' she asked, feeling like an intruder in a private world.

Jenny shook her head. 'Thanks . . . I can manage now. There's only his nasal feed to give. His wife'll be in later. Never missed a day, has she, Michael?'

Anne's next task was to relieve Don Hyde for his

coffee-break. Don had been sitting with Terry Walters, who was still not conscious after his fit.

'If he comes round before I get back, he'll probably be confused,' the charge nurse warned. 'You know . . . post-epileptic automatism.'

'Oh, yes, I'll be prepared if he comes out fighting,' said Anne, half smiling and not really expecting problems.

She had checked the patient's pulse and was about to test his pupil reflexes when there were signs of returning consciousness. He flung out his arm in an irritable manner and pushed her hands away. He mumbled incoherently, then turned himself on to his back. He stretched and yawned and scratched his head. After a few moments, while Anne waited for him to collect his wits, he opened his eyes and blinked vacantly.

'Hello, Terry, how are you feeling?' she asked in a gentle voice. Preoccupied with her patient, she was only half aware of the arrival of the doctors, being greeted by Mary in her office prior to the ward round.

Completely ignoring her, Terry sat up, determinedly pushing back the bedclothes. He then began to take off his pyjamas.

Anne took the precaution of pressing the emergency buzzer as she drew the screening curtains. 'Do you want the bathroom, Terry? Hang on a minute, love, while I get your robe,' she said. But by this time Terry had discovered that railings were keeping him confined to bed. Expressing his displeasure in loud, bawdy language, he attempted to climb over them.

She had no recourse but to try to reason with him until help arrived, but Anne's eight stone was no match for his solid frame. Roughly shoved aside, she lost her balance and would have gone sprawling had not Grant Ryder parted the curtains at that moment. Instead, she was caught in strong arms against the solid, white-coated body of the neurosurgical registrar.

'Now, what's going on here?' Grant said mildly, steadying her on her feet again and putting her to one side. 'OK, Terry, let's get you covered up. There are ladies present.'

With a tut of annoyance Mary dived into his locker and found his towelling robe. There was restrained amusement from the circle of faces around the foot of the bed and titters from nearby patients who had glimpsed the charade.

Terry was persuaded to cover his nakedness before being escorted to the toilet. He was then cajoled back to bed, Professor Drapper ordered a sedative injection, and in a little while peace reigned.

'And what about you?' Grant asked Anne. 'Anything damaged besides your dignity?'

'No, I'm fine, thank you,' she returned, more than a little bewildered at the effect of their close-quarters encounter. Goodness, if it was that devastating to be in his arms for a split second, how could anyone resist him if he made a play for them? She was glad he couldn't read her thoughts, but she couldn't stop the tell-tale colour creeping into her cheeks.

'You should have called for help earlier,' Mary reprimanded.

Professor Drapper came to her rescue by making a joke of it. 'Well, that was certainly a baptism of fire, wasn't it? I promise you, things are usually much more seemly. Now, shall we get on with the ward round, Sister?'

Later that day, when Terry had slept off the effects of his injection, he had no recollection of anything that had happened. He apologised profusely to Anne. 'Honestly, Nurse, I hardly ever use bad language, but that guy across the way said the air was *blue*!'

Anne laughed. 'Don't worry, I've heard worse. When you're not in control, it's as though all your normal restraint goes to pot. And it livened up my first day here, didn't it?' Staying to talk to him, she learned that he had never had a fit before. 'Well, you're for an EEG tomorrow, so they'll be able to tell you if there's any real problem,' she said.

He looked worried. 'Is that electric shock treatment? I don't think I want that.'

'Good heavens, no,' Anne reassured him, 'you're confusing it with ECT, which is totally different. An EEG is quite a painless test. All they do is fasten a number of little electrodes to various points on your head, and from these the electrical waves of the brain are recorded on a sheet of paper. The tracings can tell the doctors if there's anything wrong.'

He breathed a sigh of relief. 'Oh, thanks for

explaining that. Thanks a lot, Nurse. I was really worried.'

'Well, don't lose any sleep over it, there's no need,' she said kindly. 'Goodnight, Terry.'

At four-thirty she had been about to go off duty with the rest of the early shift when he had called her over. Now she was glad to be on her way. She felt tired, more mentally than physically. And there was no doubt about it that the contact with Grant, when he had saved her from falling, had been unsettling. That sensation of strength and sexuality—it was an intoxicating mixture. She was going to have to be wary. She found she was increasingly attracted to this man, whereas he showed nothing but a kind of indifference towards her.

What Anne was not prepared for on her way out was walking into Grant as she left the staff-room.

He stopped. 'Hello. So that's your first day over. And you survived. Just!' he said with a crooked smile.

'Yes, it was great,' she returned. 'I really enjoyed it, barring the odd flasher.'

His smile broadened. 'No room for false modesty in this game, my girl!'

She grinned back, wishing her heart would stop drumming. 'Terry was more embarrassed about it than I was.'

He looked across to an outside window. The rain was still falling relentlessly. Then he looked back at Anne, taking in her cagoule and umbrella. 'You cycling today?'

'No—I taxied in this morning,' she said.

He raised an equivocal eyebrow. 'Oh? That's a pricey way of getting to work. Do you do it often?'

'Depending on the weather. It's cheaper than running a car and getting hammered with parking fines. Anyway, I got a freebie this morning—for services rendered by the hospital, or so I gathered,' she told him.

He walked along with her towards the lift, pressed the button and leaned against the wall, his disconcerting blue eyes appraising her while they waited. 'I take it you will be at your sister's dinner-party on Friday?' he asked.

'Yes . . . she has asked me.' Anne swallowed and returned his narrowed gaze with innocence. 'Honestly, I knew nothing about it, until you told me the other day.'

'All right, I believe you.' His manner was teasing. 'Would you like me to provide you with transport?'

'No, thank you. I've got a half-day, so I'll probably go along earlier,' she explained.

They stepped into the lift which quickly carried them down to the ground floor.

'Brad tells me he's looking forward to it,' Grant went on.

'Does that mean that you're not? My sister knows how to entertain.'

· 'Oh, I'm sure she does. I'm sure you both do. But I don't have Brad's problem.'

She knew, from his tone of voice, that it wasn't a real problem, but out of politeness she said, 'Oh?

What's that?'

'He can't make up his mind which of the sisters he most fancies.'

She made a face at him and allowed herself a private smile. 'Then Brad is in for a disappointing evening. Michelle's motives are purely impersonal. Romance is the last thing on her mind.'

'I thought romance was never far from any girl's mind,' he countered.

'What a typically arrogant male viewpoint! It certainly doesn't tie in with the advice you threw at me during your talk last week,' she couldn't help retaliating.

'What was that? Remind me.'

'Tempering everything with your own good sense?' she retorted. 'You've no grounds for misconstruing a friendly gesture.'

Grant laughed aloud. 'The audacity of the girl, quoting my words back at me! It takes a lot to rock your little boat, doesn't it?'

'You could say that.' Anne gave him an angelic smile and walked away. And this time she didn't take a taxi. She walked in the rain to the Underground, and she walked from the Underground to the flat. It helped her to get rid of the turbulence inside her. Little did he know how near he had come to upturning her little boat in a stormy sea.

The following day, with Mary taking time off because her little boy had tonsillitis, and with no more help forthcoming, there was extra work for all to do. Don Hyde took charge and enjoyed doing so, although he grumbled good-humouredly about the additional responsibility thrust upon him.

'There's some post for Mr Carle. Take it along, will you?' he said to Anne when she came back from her tea-break. 'I'm not dancing attendance on private patients.'

'He has to pay his insurance like everyone else,' Anne pointed out mildly. 'If he likes to pay twice, who are we to grumble?'

Don thought about that for a moment. 'Yes, you may be right. A bloke's entitled to spend his bread how he likes. But I can't stand the way Mary fusses over him.'

Anne nipped along with the letters. She hadn't seen Alistair Carle since the day of his operation and she welcomed the opportunity to find out how he was faring. With a light tap on the door, she entered with a smile. It faded a little when she discovered both Grant and Bob Ramsgate there with the patient.

'Oh, excuse me,' she murmured. 'Your afternoon post,' she went on, addressing the man sitting by the side of his bed in a paisley silk dressing-gown.

Alistair Carle was a small man with sharp dark eyes in a thinnish face. No bandage on his head now. Dark hair was beginning to sprout where it had been shaven before the craniotomy, and the bruising around his eyes had begun to fade.

'Thank you, Nurse.' He eyed her trim figure in the saxe-blue uniform. 'I don't think we've met before?'

'Oh, yes, you have,' put in Grant, 'although you were not aware of it at the time. Nurse Westlake was in theatre when we were sorting out your brains.'

'Really?' The patient's eyes twinkled. 'I hope you made sure that they put them back in the right order.'

Anne laughed. 'I'm afraid I played a very minor role in that. But it's good to see you looking so well, Mr Carle.'

'Yes.' He smiled his gratitude all round. 'I've much to be thankful for. Mr Ryder tells me I should be as good as new, providing I take life quietly for a time.'

Another knock on the door interrupted their conversation.

'Is this a private party, or may I join in?' a cultured voice enquired playfully.

Anne turned at the familiar accent, and her mouth gaped slightly to find Jonathan Locke—immaculately attired as always—pausing on the threshold.

Mr Carle beckoned him in. 'My dear chap, how nice of you to come. We're only chatting. Come and meet my good friends.'

Jonathan promptly bounded across to Anne and kissed her on both cheeks. 'I know this one very well. I hope you're not working our Anne too hard,' he said, beaming at the doctors.

'*Our* Anne?' Grant frowned at this unexpected display of affection, clearly not remembering

Jonathan from the Barbican evening.

'It's all right, sir,' Jonathan laughed, 'I'm a friend of the family. In fact we both know her father, don't we, Alistair?'

Mr Carle's eyebrows shot up while his gaze registered the name-badge on Anne's uniform. 'Oh, so you're Sir Randolph's daughter!' he exclaimed, recognition dawning. 'I must remember to thank him for providing one of the ministering angels.'

She felt it was high time to make herself scarce. She smiled and picked up his afternoon tea-tray. 'My father had precious little to do with it. I'll get rid of this for you.'

Jonathan leapt to open the door for her as she made her exit. 'What time are you free?' he asked confidentially. 'Could we go for a meal?'

'Sorry, Jon,' she said, 'I'm not off until nine-thirty.'

'Oh, pity,' he sighed. 'I must get Belinda to invite you over when she's feeling more herself.'

By the time she had deposited the tray in the kitchen Anne had given way to a fair bit of colourful language herself. Of all the rotten luck, Jon showing up like that! He could be talkative, and she could imagine all her family's affairs being brought out for viewing after she left. Not that there was anything to hide, but she didn't relish being the subject of medical common-room gossip.

The main ward was now well peopled with visitors and there was time to catch up with routine chores. Don asked Anne to check the stock requisition and put the goods away.

She was in the store-room, putting sterile packs in the neatly-kept pigeon holes, when Grant wandered in.

'When you've finished that,' he said, 'if you'll come to the office I'd like to talk about Terry Walters, since you were the first person to see him fitting.'

'OK,' she said, 'I'll be five minutes.'

He had the patient's notes open in front of him and was busily writing when she joined him.

'Sit down.' He indicated the chair beside him, wrote for another minute, then turned to look at her. 'Now, how good were your powers of observation? What can you tell me that I don't already know? What kind of a fit do you think it could have been—Jacksonian?'

Dismissing all personal thoughts from her head, Anne cast her mind back to her arrival on the scene the previous morning. 'I can't say. The convulsions were generalised when I arrived. They lasted two minutes. He did look cyanosed. Sister Mary tested his pupillary reflexes and said they were absent.' She went on to report everything else she could remember and finished by saying that Terry had been worried about the EEG. 'He was confusing it with electro-convulsive therapy until I explained the difference.'

Grant smiled at her and shook his head. 'I wish patients would ask *me* questions. One doesn't always think to explain in detail. Anyway, you set his mind at rest?'

'Yes, I think so. Have you come to any conclusions yet?'

He scratched his cheek thoughtfully. 'It may be cerebral scarring—he was unconscious after a road accident a few years back. We must have a CAT scan, I think.' He closed the notes.

'Well, if that's all . . .' Anne stood up, anxious to conclude the interview.

'Yes, that's all, Anne. Except to say that your friend, Mr Locke, seems all set to act as bookie's runner for our Mr Carle. Racing is *not* the best kind of preoccupation for a peaceful convalescence,' Grant remarked disapprovingly.

'Oh, well, that's none of my business,' Anne declared. 'And Jonathan's not really *my friend*, as you put it. I expect he told you I used to work for him.'

Grant's austere manner suddenly softened. 'Yes,' he said. 'He also mentioned that you lost your mother in rather tragic circumstances. I'm sorry about that.'

Tears suddenly blinded Anne's eyes. She hadn't cried about it for some time, but sympathy from this unexpected quarter caught her off-guard. She buried her face in her hands until the awful moment passed. There were still times when she missed her mother dreadfully.

Grant's normally detached expression gave way to remorse. 'Anne, that was really stupid of me.' Pushing back his chair, he came to put comforting hands on her shoulders. 'I should have known . . . it hurts for ages.'

'As if you care!' she flared, angrily dashing away her tears and shaking herself free of his attempt at sympathy. 'People are here today and gone tomorrow—it happens all the time.'

He put his spurned hands in his pockets, giving her a moment to control herself. 'Yes, it's happening all the time,' he agreed quietly, 'but I prevent it when I can, and it saddens me when I can't. Am I forgiven?'

She found a tissue in her pocket and blew her nose vigorously, now feeling like a prize idiot to have let go. 'I shan't be, if I don't get on,' she returned with an attempt at flippancy. 'I should be helping Jenny with Michael.' Fleeing back to the stock-room, she found a clean tissue and had another good blow before joining the other staff nurse in the high-dependency unit.

'Oh, there you are,' said Jenny, and giving her a second look, 'You all right?'

'Yes, fine. Just a bit of hay fever . . . the pollen count's high today. Good job we don't get a lot of flowers in here.'

After changing his position, they were gently creaming Michael's pressure areas when there was a throaty kind of sound.

The nurses paused and looked at each other.

'That wasn't you, was it?' Jenny's eyes strayed to Michael's face with the Ryle's tube in one nostril and his tracheostomy connected to the ventilator.

Anne was wide-eyed. 'No! It must have been him!'

In the next instant there was no doubt that the

patient was making noises in his throat. He was also making a feeble attempt to lift his arm—the one with the intravenous infusion line splinted to it. His eyelids fluttered open.

'He's coming round,' gulped Jenny. 'He's trying to breathe for himself!' She took her patient's hand in hers. 'Michael . . . you're in hospital . . . you had a bad accident . . . try not to struggle against the tubes . . .' To Anne, she hissed, 'Get Grant!'

Anne flew. She caught the registrar as he was about to leave the ward.

'Alleluia!' he murmured, returning with rapid strides. 'Give the anaesthetist a buzz, will you? The ventilator's his province.'

Georges Alain arrived, and news began to trickle through to the ward. The man in the special room was coming out of his coma! Everyone was thrilled. Even Millic, the slow-footed ward maid whisked the supper trays around in breezy good humour.

Jenny went off at four-thirty, so that it was Anne who was privileged to witness the joy of Michael's wife when she arrived to see him that evening.

His bed had been pumped up to a sitting position, and though he was still attached to tubes and machines, his eyes were open and perceptive, following Anne around the room as she filled in his charts and checked that everything was as it should be.

'Did they tell you you'd been here four weeks?' said Anne, smiling at him after moistening his mouth with a cool wet swab. 'And your wife has been in to see you every day. It's going to be a wonderful surprise for her to find you awake.'

Michael's wife arrived two hours later.

She paused on the threshold. Her hands flew to her mouth. 'Oh, Mike!' she choked, her face crumpling.

Anne's eyes filled too. 'Isn't it great?' she said, putting an arm around the girl's shoulders and giving her a hug. 'It happened this afternoon, but we couldn't get hold of you to tell you. It will take a little while to get him properly weaned off the ventilator and to get full control of his functions. But he's going to be fine. Mr Ryder will be here presently. He'll tell you all about it.'

Pulling out a chair for the visitor, she left them together for a moment while she went to get Michael's evening drugs and have them checked.

You'll never guess what's happened!' wailed Michelle, ringing Anne at the flat at eleven o'clock the following night. 'Someone let the bath overflow upstairs, and it's brought down the ceiling in my living-room. You never *saw* such a mess!'

'Oh, my gosh! That's awkward.' Anne paused. 'What are you going to do, then? Will you have to call off your dinner-party?'

'Good heavens, no! First of all I did wonder if we could use your place, but it's such a dump. So I decided to ask Daddy, and he says I can use home. He'll sleep at his club that night. Isn't he a pet?'

'Yes, he is,' Anne agreed. 'What about the

caterers, will they deliver to South Ken?'

'Oh, yes, no problem, and there'll be more room in the kitchen for them. Now my only hang-up is letting Grant and Brad know about the change of place. I had such awful trouble getting Grant on the phone the other day—so I'll leave that to you. I mean, you see Grant practically every day, don't you?'

Privately Anne groaned. She had no wish to go seeking out the registrar to talk about dinner-parties. After her pathetic breakdown the other day she felt highly embarrassed whenever she saw him. But it was a perfectly logical request on Michelle's part, so there was nothing she could do about it. 'OK,' she said, 'I'm bound to see one of them before Friday.'

It was so stupid to be worried about such a little thing, but Anne found herself rehearsing the best way of saying it. In the end she wrote out the address and carried it around in her uniform pocket so as to be able to hand it over with the least possible fuss when the opportunity arose.

As it turned out, nothing could have been easier. With Sister Mary still absent, the atmosphere was more relaxed in the ward under Don Hyde's easy-going but still efficient management.

Grant came up in his theatre garb, having operated successfully on a spinal tumour. After seeing his patient safely bedded, he threw out a plea, 'How about a coffee for a hard-working surgeon?'

'Sure. You'll make it, will you, Annie?' said

Don.

Anne trooped off to do so and took it to Grant in the doctor's office. She also pulled out her father's address from her pocket and laid it on the desk in front of him.

'Michelle's ceiling fell down,' she explained, 'so the party on Friday will be at my father's house, there. Not quite so far to go,' she smiled. 'OK?'

'Chatswood Gardens, South Kensington,' he read slowly, and looked up at her. 'Was that where you grew up?'

'Only partly. We had a place in Kent until my mother died.' She saw a flicker of unease in his attentive blue eyes, and laughed. 'Don't worry, I'm not going to go to pieces again. You caught me in a fit of the blues the other day.'

He smiled in relief. 'My fault, I shouldn't have mentioned it.'

'For goodness' sake, I'm a big girl now,' she joked, and left him with his coffee. That had gone rather well, she felt, *and* helped to salvage her dignity.

CHAPTER FIVE

IN HER large kitchen in Chatswood Gardens Lilian Mackay—or 'Mrs Mac' as she was popularly known—finished polishing the silver and filled the electric kettle for a cup of tea. She always made it in the pot; she couldn't stand this tea-bag-in-the-cup stuff. And in any case, one of the girls might be here by the time the water boiled.

Mrs Mac had been with the family many years now. She had started in Lamberhurst when the girls were growing up and her own Billy had gone off to Australia to make his fortune, promising to send for her. He never did. Since then the Westlakes had been her family and she had seen them through the good and the bad times.

She remembered the fuss when Anne—the youngest—had thrown up her cushy job at the Gallery and gone nursing, bless her. And there was Michelle's wonderful wedding, and that awful time when her husband had turned out to be gay. Mac was glad her ladyship hadn't lived to see that.

Ever since the accident Mrs Mac had run this gracious house as if it were her own, with the aid of a woman for the rough. She arranged the flowers which still came weekly from the local florist. She polished the beautiful furniture, she shopped for Sir Randolph, she washed and ironed his clothes, polished his shoes and would even have supplied personal comforts if he had wanted it. But Sir Randolph was a real gent. He would never take liberties, even if she were thirty years younger and interested in such things, which she wasn't. But that didn't stop her adoring every hair on his polished silver head.

As for the daughters, both lovely girls they were, although Michelle was always the flighty one. Now Anne, there was a lass you'd be glad to call your own.

Mrs Mac wondered what this dinner party was in aid of. Sir Randolph had only said something about Michelle needing to have the workmen in, which was why they were coming here.

On hearing a taxi draw up outside, she looked through the basement window and saw Anne alight. The housekeeper hastened up the small flight of stairs to open the door to the daughter of the house, clad in jeans and lightweight blouson, her lustrous fair hair lifting in the breeze.

'Hello, Mac,' Anne exclaimed affectionately, bounding up the steps with her holdall. She greeted the worthy Scotswoman with a kiss. 'How's the old knee, then? Any better?'

'Not bad, lass. I got some new pills from the doctor, but he says the best thing is to lose a bit of weight. I'm just brewing tea . . . will you take a cup?'

'Yes, please, and a drop scone, if you've got any made, Mac. I came straight from the hospital and I'm starving. Mustn't spoil my appetite for tonight, though.'

'I made some specially, this morning,' said the housekeeper, pleased.

Anne paused to admire the great bowl of stocks, cream roses and butterfly gladioli on a pedestal in the hall. 'Lovely flowers,' she said, following down into the kitchen. 'You've developed a real flair for arranging them.'

'Thank you, dear. Those classes I went to taught me a lot.' The housekeeper made the tea, set the dainty Wedgwood cups on a tray and produced a plate of her famous drop scones and butter.

They sat exchanging gossip for a time before the older woman said, 'So you'll not be needing my help tonight, then, if Michelle's got these caterers coming?'

'That's right. They bring everything with them—the plates, the cutlery, the glasses, the lot. Terrific, isn't it?'

The housekeeper sniffed. 'I would've done it, you know.'

'I know you would—but it was all laid on already. So you just find the mats for the table—there'll be six of us—then you can disappear. We'll be fine.'

'What are you giving them to eat?'

'Michelle made the choice.' Anne thought for a moment. 'I think it's going to be smoked salmon mousse, followed by Chicken Kiev with mushrooms, broccoli, Lyonnaise potatoes, and fresh fruit Pavlova for dessert.'

'Sounds all right,' the housekeeper approved. 'Good thing you girls don't have to watch your weight.'

Anne's laugh rang out. 'Let's hope it's as good as it sounds! Well, I'm going to have my bath now and try to make up my mind what to wear.'

Mrs Mac gathered up the cups and saucers to wash. 'Any of these young men important to you, dear?' she enquired casually over her shoulder.

Anne smiled. 'Oh, no . . . it's really a business thing. Some people from Mich's office and a couple of doctors from the hospital whom she wants to interest in a project. You know Mich . . . always thinking three steps ahead.'

Skipping up to her own room, she sorted through the many clothes in the wardrobe and decided there were lots she ought to throw out. She didn't need an excess of smart things these days. Parties and socials in hospital circles were far from the glamorous affairs she used to attend. She enjoyed them all the more for that—the people were warmer, less superficial.

Tonight, however, she wanted to be—well—ornamental. Michelle had gone to a lot of trouble setting this up for her own purposes, although admittedly having it at Chatswood Gardens was not what she had planned. Whether or not her sister's ideas came off, Anne determined to do her best to make the party sparkle. Of course, it might also make the lofty Grant Ryder sit up and take notice, which couldn't be bad.

Psyching herself up to play the role of socialite again, she chose a deceptively simple ivory silk designer dress. It had the narrowest of shoulder straps and a decorative soft pink leather belt to clasp about her waist. Matching pink evening sandals completed her outfit.

Michelle arrived with a new frock she had bought for the occasion—a slinky model in midnight-blue crêpe, discreetly enhancing her seductive figure. As always she was the picture of elegance.

'Oh, that's gorgeous!' said Anne, going into her sister's room to cadge some pink nail varnish. 'You'll wow them in that!'

'Off to a good start,' Michelle returned, giving a graceful pirouette on her high heels. Her rich dark hair was combed into careful disorder. 'Charm 'em into submission, that's my plan. You look great too. The perfect English rose,' she clowned. 'Brad Stevens will go mad for you.'

'Idiot!' Anne laughed. It certainly wasn't Brad she was out to impress!

The two young women from the catering firm were by now busy in the kitchen and Mrs Mac, having shown them around, had disappeared to her own quarters.

Michelle took a yellow pill from the small box on her dressing-table, popped it into her mouth and went to the bathroom for a drink of water.

'What are you taking now?' Anne frowned, waving her lacquered nails to dry.

'Just something to boost my morale. I might seem the most together person on two legs, but I'm really not,' her sister said. 'I get battalions of butterflies in my stomach at the drop of a hat.'

'Well, watch it—those things are addictive. Don't just pop them into your mouth whenever. You could get hooked.'

Michelle made a face in the mirror while fastening on her chandelier earrings. 'Back off, Annie,' she said petulantly. 'There's a lot of pressure in my job. You don't know the half of it.'

'Sorry . . . but I'm worried about you, Michy. If the job's that stressful why do you put up with it?'

'Don't be stupid!' her sister flared. 'I love it. Besides, I *have* to succeed at something. I made a mess of choosing a husband, didn't I?'

'OK, OK, only trying to help,' Anne said mildly. 'Come on, let's go down and sort out the drinks.'

Their guests arrived within minutes of each other. Michelle's producer Joe Casey and his assistant, Hilary, came by taxi, and the two doctors in Grant's modest Ford Escort. They had made their own introductions on the doorstep by the time the girls answered their ring at the door.

'Well, do come in,' Michelle invited brightly. 'Hi, Joe . . . Hilary. This is my sister Anne. She works with these two . . .'

Kissing seemed to be the order of the day. Anne found herself being saluted on the cheek by Joe, and Brad, and lastly Grant.

Their eyes met as they drew away, his faintly puckish, hers wide and wondering. For a moment no one else existed. She forgot that she had intended to be the life and soul of the party. She forgot everything except a wish for something more than their cheeks brushing. His gaze told her she was desirable, but there was also something enigmatic in his expression, a look she could not fathom. One thing she did know—it would take no effort on her part to fall for this aggravating, austere, attractive man.

It was Brad who set her in motion again. 'Lovely place you have here,' he exclaimed, looking about him in the hall and taking in the curving staircase with its decorative wrought-iron banisters. His gaze rose to the ceiling. 'Gee, what wouldn't some of the folks back home give for that fancy plasterwork! How old are these places?'

Anne found her voice. 'Georgian, I think,' she said absently. 'Come into the conservatory . . . we're having drinks in there.'

Everyone integrated remarkably well. Joe, a big bear of a man, had dark eyes which darted everywhere. Anne could see them recording impressions like a computer, while Hilary, his personal assistant, was ready to agree with everything he said. She was a quiet, mousy girl, swamped by his personality. Although he must have been well over forty and she in her twenties, it was obvious they were having an affair.

'Why aren't you in the kitchen with your pinny on?' Joe demanded suddenly during a lull in the small-talk, his eyes savouring Michelle's well-groomed appearance. 'I didn't know you were this well organised.'

'I have hidden depths you know not of,' she returned, her laughter rippling. 'Actually, I decided to spoil you tonight, on account of our American friend. I couldn't inflict my abysmal cooking on Brad, so I've hired some people I know.'

'God, how the poor live!' scoffed Joe.

Anne could not help noticing the sardonic twist which played about the corners of Grant's lips.

Michelle's faith in her caterers was well justified. The meal was a triumph, beautifully presented, and the cooks unobtrusive. The guests grew relaxed and happy. Brad Stevens was a good raconteur. He had a certain irreverence for his elders and betters and kept the table entertained with his tales of medical *faux pas* in America.

'What about you, Grant, have you ever screwed it up?' asked Joe.

'I wouldn't be telling *you* if I had,' the surgeon retorted with a half-smile. 'To have it dissected on one of your trial-by-TV programmes? No, thanks! Seriously, and fingers crossed,' he went on, darting a mischievous glance at Anne, 'there's nothing on my conscience to date, except perhaps intimidating a few ham-fisted students who won't be making the same mistakes twice.'

Joe's eyes slid towards Anne. 'Does he intimidate the nurses as well?'

'Ask me that in six months' time,' she grinned. 'I'm bearing up so far.'

It wasn't until they were served with coffee in the luxurious sitting-room that the subject of the current affairs programme was broached.

'We'll be doing a one-off on the state of the Health Service shortly,' said Joe, lighting up a small cheroot and blowing smoke in the air.

'There'll be a panel of experts and an invited audience of interested parties. What do you think's wrong with it?' he demanded, looking directly at Grant.

'A pretty sweeping question, that.' The registrar scratched his cheek thoughtfully. 'Nothing much that money couldn't put right. The trouble is, the more medical science advances, the more costly it becomes. Everyone clamours for more funds from the Government, but the Government has only one source of income, and that's the taxpayer.'

'Yah,' nodded Joe ponderously, 'your average citizen seems to forget that.'

'People are very generous when it comes to fund-raising,' Anne defended. 'It would be a pity to change our system and lose that goodwill.'

Grant warmed to his subject. 'Yes, the public is great when it come to special appeals. But they don't realise the ongoing costs of everyday things like X-Rays, and blood tests, etc. And the drugs bill is phenomenal, let alone the wages.' He paused to sip his coffee. 'Strikes within the service over internal problems are a pity . . . all they do is create misery for everyone.'

Michelle stole a lively glance at the producer.

'So what's your solution?' asked Joe.

'I don't really know,' the registrar said. 'I'm no financial expert, but I do know medicine has an insatiable appetite. It's like a cuckoo in a robin's nest. It could eat up everything and still want more.' He shrugged and smiled. 'That's not very constructive, is it? Perhaps the only answer is in better housekeeping . . . and patience . . . and an appreciation of what has been achieved. We've come a long way even if there's still a lot to be done!'

'Ha! I like your attitude.' Joe slapped his knee. 'Come and say it on the box. Would you care to fish out a few facts and figures and join the panel?'

Grant shook his head determinedly. 'Thanks, but no, thanks. I'm not heavyweight enough to be sounding off in public. Ask me in a few years' time, when I've got a consultancy under my belt. But I might be able to put you in touch with someone . . . or how about Brad here, to compare our lot with the Americans? I'm sure he wouldn't object to a bit of public exposure,' he grinned.

'Hey, don't drop me in it,' Brad protested.

The conversation ranged back and forth with everyone airing their views. It was midnight before the producer and his secretary departed, leaving it that Grant would put out feelers for a suitable contact for the programme.

'Oh, Grant, you disappointed me,' Michelle pouted. 'You would have been a tremendous hit, I know.'

He laughed and playfully ruffled her hair. 'I don't want to be a hit, I'm happy with being a surgeon.' He looked from one sister to the other, his eyes narrowing. 'Did you two cook this meeting up with this in mind?'

'Well, it was me really, and only partly,' Michelle admitted. 'I did also want to show Brad a good time. You two don't need to go yet, do you? Why don't we have some dancing?' She went to the music centre and put on a tape.

Brad was left with no choice in the matter as to which sister he would dance with. Grant commandeered Anne, putting both arms around her slim body as a haunting melody by Andrew Lloyd Webber played.

The men had earlier discarded their jackets, and long before the tape finished, Anne found herself ever more tightly pressed against Grant's strong, virile body. Sensations burned through the silk of her dress. Every inch of her seemed merged with him in a white-hot incandescence. She laid her head against his chest while they moved to the music. She felt his lips on her hair. From there it took but the briefest turn of their heads for his mouth to find hers, and soon tortuous longings were flooding her being. This was like nothing she'd ever known. And if actions spoke louder than words, she felt it was the same for him too.

Her sister and Brad were having fun, noisily enjoying themselves. When the music came to an end, Michelle flung herself on the sofa and yawned widely. Brad leaned over her, put his finger in her open mouth and tickled her tongue. 'You have the sweetest tonsils,' he said.

She giggled. 'I had them out when I was five. Hey, stop smooching, you two!' she called, turning to the others.

Reluctantly Grant released Anne. 'Yes, we ought to be going now. Are you both staying here ... or could I drop anyone anywhere?'

'I'm staying,' said Michelle, 'I want to go to Harrods in the morning. How about you, Annie?'

'No, I'm on at one-thirty tomorrow, so I'd be glad of a lift back, if you wouldn't mind, Grant?'

'Fine. Ready when you are,' he said.

Her eyes were luminous as she smiled up at him. 'I'll just go and collect my gear.'

Humming the melody that still lingered in her head, Anne ran up to her room, shoved jeans and trainers into her holdall, picked up her shoulder-bag and went back to the sitting-room where the others were waiting.

'Sorry to leave you on your own, Mich. You don't mind?'

'I'd be alone if I went back to Hampstead.' her sister pointed out. 'Go on, I'll be fine.'

'How about me staying to keep you company?' suggested Brad.

Michelle drew him to her by the lapels and kissed him. 'Nothing I should like better, *but* . . . what I should like and what is advisable are two different things. Besides, my father's housekeeper would be shocked. Goodnight, Brad.'

'Pity,' he sighed. 'Thanks for a lovely party, honey. I'll be in touch.'

'Yes, thank you,' said Grant. 'I enjoyed it too, it was tremendous. Sorry about the programme, but I'll find you someone better than me.'

Anne kissed her sister goodbye and soon they were driving through Knightsbridge on the way to the City.

Grant dropped Brad back at his rooms before making the detour to Finsbury with Anne.

'And will you be on your own tonight?' he asked when he drew to a halt outside the Victorian terraced house she had pointed out.

'Apart from the couple upstairs, yes.' She explained about her flatmate's accident on the beach.

'Oh, nasty.' Grant drummed with his fingers on the steering wheel, his glance taking in the shabby neighbourhood. 'This is a far cry from the things you're used it, isn't it?'

She smiled. 'You can get used to anything. Anyway, it's the people, not buildings, that matter.'

He rested an arm along the back of her seat and turned to look at her, his shadowed features inscrutable.'True . . . but who'd live in a slum if they could live in a palace?'

'I've never lived in a palace, so I wouldn't know,' she replied pertly. 'Have you.'

He chuckled. 'I've lived practically everywhere else. But don't let's waste the witching hour talking about bricks and mortar. Time you kissed me goodnight, Miss Westlake.'

Her heart pumped urgently. She ran her tongue along her bottom lip as she drew a halting breath, putting off the magic moment. 'You don't want to come in for coffee?'

He stroked her bare, slender arm and murmured, 'Now, do you think that would be a good idea? I think your sister was right. Let's part while I still have a modicum of control.' Drawing her to him, he teased her lips with his and, finding her responsive, became more adventurous. It tested her powers of restraint to the utmost. Heavens above, how could such pleasure be such pain?

'Y-you're right,' she said, with a shaky laugh when he drew away. 'I think that's enough for one night. Goodbye.' With a swift smile she let herself out of the car and ran indoors. Lying against the front door as she quietly closed it, Anne knew that she was more helplessly committed than she had ever been in her life before. She was filled with an excited kind of expectancy. He had wanted her, that was obvious, but he had respected her too much to press it. Surely that augured well for the future? Anne hugged herself with delight.

Having decided to lunch in the hospital canteen, Anne set off for work at midday on Saturday. It was a pearl of a morning as she made for the Underground. The weather was grand and all the passers-by seemed in good spirits—unless that was a reflection of her own blissful state of mind. She doubted whether Grant would be in over the weekend, barring emergencies. And on Monday and Tuesday she had days off, which would make it mid-week before they saw each other again. But that was only happiness deferred.

Even the posse of protesting workers at the main gates of the hospital failed to depress her. They were mostly domestic staff, brandishing placards proclaiming their grievances about cuts in staffing levels, but there were a number of nurses among them lending support.

On reaching the canteen she met up with Hazel, of whom she'd seen little since they started work. They sat down at a table together with their cottage cheese salads, doughnuts and coffee.

'And what makes you so cheerful?' Hazel asked, buttering her roll. 'Didn't you get pressured to join the demo?'

'Oh, I slipped by,' Anne said. 'Not that I don't sympathise if they've got a real beef, but I refuse to be dictated to by the militants.'

Hazel agreed. 'Personally, I think *all* the public services should be accountable and have no-strike clauses. Then you'd know where you were and if you didn't like it you shouldn't join. I mean, this holding the public to ransom to get what you want . . . it's positively uncivilised!' She took a savage bite of her doughnut.

Anne laughed. 'That got that off your chest! Well, if it does come to strike action it'll be emergency cover only and extra work for us. Good thing we've got no one desperately ill at the moment. Although that could change at any time.'

'Yeah, we'll just have to get on with it, as usual, I suppose. Guess what,' Hazel went on, dropping the thorny subject, 'Don's arranged a rounders match for tomorrow evening—us versus Jenner Ward—if you're on an early. I'm not.'

'Rounders!' Anne chuckled. 'I haven't played that since I was at school. He's a real live wire, Don, isn't he?'

The two girls went up to the ward together,

talking shop. Hazel was thrilled because the patient she'd been specialling—the man whose spinal neurofibroma Grant had successfully removed—had begun to get the feeling back in his legs.

'And how's our Michael . . . is he doing OK?' asked Anne.

'Fine, I believe. Jenny and his wife had a little weep together last night. She'd just had it confirmed she was pregnant, and she'd been thinking he might never live to know the baby.'

Anne felt emotion sweeping over her again. 'Terrific,' she sighed. 'That's one of Grant's *hoorays,* isn't it?'

They went to the staff-room to leave their belongings.

In the ward there was the usual bustle of routine procedures which had to be got through before visitors could be allowed in. With many patients coming from outer London, visiting at the weekend was always heavier than on weekdays. Once the work was done the nurses would have a little time to themselves to catch up on paperwork and other chores.

Reporting to the office for duty, Anne found Sister Mary once more in charge, wearing her customary harassed look.

'Nice to see you back, Sister,' Anne said. 'Is your little boy better?'

'Well, not a hundred per cent, but my husband is there weekends.' Mary sighed. 'It's fine being a working mum when everything's OK, but how

often is that? If only my mother lived next door!'
She picked up the internal phone when it rang,
spoke briefly and put it down again. 'That was
Grant . . . asking for Terry Walters' case notes. Fish
them out and take them in, will you, Annie?'

A frisson ran down Anne's spine as she heard
that Grant was present. She quickly thumbed
through the case-notes trolley. 'I didn't think he'd
be in today.'

'Yes, he's in his office with Dr Arbuthnot and
Brad Stevens. They're trying to get ahead because
of this threatened strike by the ancillary workers.
Oh, by the way,' Mary consulted the off-duty
roster, 'if it comes about, you won't be able to have
those days off. We shall need all the hands we can
get. Do you mind?' She darted a glance at Anne.
'Unless, of course, you were planning to join
them?'

'Me?' Anne returned. 'I detest the whole
degrading, upsetting business!' She found what she
was looking for and lifted out the file.

'At least we got rid of Mr Carle before the
balloon goes up. He left this morning . . . and gave
us that,' Mary added, nodding towards two bottles
of champagne and a large box of chocolates on top
of the filing cabinet, 'although goodness knows
when we'll have time for celebrating. Which
reminds me, there's still his room to get cleaned
out.'

She would have carried on talking had not Anne
interrupted. 'I'd better get this along to Grant,
hadn't I?' she said.

'Can't think what's the matter with his own legs,' the sister grumbled. 'These doctors! They think we're here just to dance attendance on them. When you've done that there are those stitches to take out of Alan Riley's scalp wound. I'm going to a staff meeting, if anyone wants to know where I am.'

This time Anne didn't mind dancing attendance. She waltzed along to the doctor's office and held out the folder with a smile. 'You wanted Terry Walters' case notes.'

Grant, sitting at his desk with the other two doctors beside him, barely glanced up as he took the file. 'Thank you. You took your time,' he snapped.

Anne could hardly believe it. Was this the warm and loving man who had held and kissed her last night? She bit back the urge to explode and coolly consulted the pendant watch pinned to her blue uniform. 'I came on duty at one-thirty. It is now only one-thirty-five, so I hardly think you can accuse *me* of wasting time.'

Grant was for the moment lost for words. Dr Arbuthnot wiped a smile from his round face and Brad chuckled.

'That told you, buddy,' the American said, and, clasping his hands behind his sandy head, he winked at Anne unashamedly.

The registrar was unsmiling. 'All right,' he said, 'I admit it was Mary I spoke to last . . . but that was the second time of asking.'

That, evidently, was all the apology she was likely to get. Anne marched out on her dignity, although she could have cried.

He had treated her like some remiss first-year student. Certainly not like a senior staff nurse, and one he'd been more than friendly with the night before. It was like a slap in the face, a staggering anticlimax after what had been between them. Go to hell, Grant Ryder, she thought stormily, I'm not having you blow hot and cold when it suits you!

She went to search out Alan Riley in order to get on with the next job. Alan was a lad of eighteen who had come off worst in a pub brawl. He had been unconscious for a few hours after being slashed with a knife and kicked in the head. Since he was of no fixed abode it was decided to keep him in until his stitches could be removed.

Anne found him in the day-room where he sat slumped in front of the television, in a hospital dressing-gown. He was a leggy youth, not bad looking in spite of his bruises, but with an air of defeatism about him. She knew something of his history. He was one of those bits of life's flotsam she felt so powerless to do anything about.

'Alan,' she said with a friendly smile, 'if you'll come with me to the treatment-room I'll take your stitches out. Then Mr Ryder will give you your marching orders, I expect.'

He rose when she spoke to him, and trooped along beside her. 'Chuckin' out time, is it?' he said. 'Pity . . . I was gettin' used to three meals a day.'

Anne laughed. 'What will you do? Go back to your squat, or go back home for a while?'

'Go back to Manchester? Don't make me laugh!

My stepfather booted me out as soon as I left school. They don't want me there.'

She got out a suture-removal pack and asked him to lie down on the couch. She could see him tense and his hands begin to ball into fists.

'Relax, Alan. It's not going to hurt . . . you won't feel a thing. Have you seen our social worker?' She carried on talking, lifting a knot with her tweezers, snipping the catgut and expertly removing a stitch. 'She might be able to help you. Or what about Father Dooley . . . you're a Catholic, aren't you?'

'My mum was. I'm nothing. No, I'll be all right, don't you worry about me,' he boasted.

One by one she removed the stitches from the long slash across his scalp. 'Now look, Alan,' she said firmly, 'we haven't patched you up so that you can go out and get into more trouble. Why don't you try to make something of yourself? Don't just drift. You're intelligent, and at the moment you're healthy. Have you tried to get a job?'

'Well, not lately . . . I gave up.'

'Well, *don't!*' she scolded him. 'How about trying the services? My dad was in the Army, and he did all right.' She omitted to say her father had been a colonel in the Grenadier Guards. 'You'd learn a trade, and get some money behind you, *plus* your three meals a day.'

They were laughing together about that when Grant Ryder came into the room to inspect the wound. 'May I see? Yes, that looks good, son. What was the joke just now?'

The boy grinned. 'Aw . . . she was telling me to

join the Army, like her dad.'

Clearing away her equipment, Anne had turned her back on Grant when he entered, so she missed the slightly comic expression on his face. 'Well, you could do a lot worse than her dad,' he agreed. 'OK, you can go home when you're ready. And stay out of fights, will you?'

The boy went back to the day-room to await the arrival of his mates.

Grant stayed in the treatment-room, leaning against the couch, watching Anne's quick, neat movements as she tidied up and washed her hands.

'We're sending Terry Walters home too,' he said. 'The CAT scan confirmed cerebral scarring, but we're not considering surgery for the time being. His fit was undoubtedly caused by this latest fall aggravating old scar tissue. It may never happen again.'

'Oh, really? Good,' Anne returned distantly. 'Was there something else . . . or may I get on with my work?'

They exchanged glances—hers inimical, his probing.

'What's biting you?' he demanded.

Her eyes widened in protest. 'I don't know how you can ask that . . . after being so churlish to me!'

'Churlish . . . *me*? I was merely stating facts, or so I thought. Admittedly you took the rap for someone else, but I had a lot on my mind.'

'Then you should have said so and apologised.'

'All right—I apologise. Does that suit you?' He gave her his bone-melting smile. 'Come on, let's be friends. I can't stand atmospheres. I thought you were on your high horse because I kissed you last night.'

'I thought you'd forgotten you had,' she said.

'That's not so easily forgotten,' he returned with a rakish grin. 'When I'm old and lonely I shall take that memory out and view it with nostalgia.'

She didn't know quite where all this was leading, but she was seduced by his charm. 'Oh, shucks,' she joked, and laughed. 'Why are you so sure you're going to be old and lonely?'

Grant dug his hands in his pockets, looking soulful. 'Because the woman I want is out of my reach.'

Anne had the feeling he meant it. 'Funny thing . . . I thought that once about a man I knew. But I grew out of it. There'll be someone else along before you reach retirement.'

'No, I shall die an embittered bachelor.'

Now she knew he was simply being facetious.

'Then I shall waste no more good advice on you,' she retorted in the same flippant manner. But there was a song in her heart as she went back to her work. They were friends, and wasn't that the best sort of beginning for any relationship?

CHAPTER SIX

MARY came back from her staff meeting that afternoon looking more harassed than ever. 'The talks have failed,' she told everyone, 'the strike's on from Monday.'

Millie, their ward maid, took round afternoon teas, apologising to the patients that it had nothing to do with her, but she had to go along with the rest or be called names. 'Still, don't you worry,' she told them, 'there's bound to be someone to make you a cuppa.'

Don cancelled his proposed rounders match between Fleming and Jenner Wards. No one could arouse any enthusiasm for that at the moment.

It was almost like a state of siege at the hospital with the preparations that needed to be made. The operating-rooms would be closed, except for emergencies, therefore patients for pre-planned surgery had to be contacted and put off. Nursing officers checked up on which of the nursing staff proposed to support the strike. Dieticians worried about food arrangements, doctors worried about their patients, and the director of nursing services worried about everything,

Anne should have been on the afternoon shift that Monday, but she had volunteered to put in extra time, knowing there would be much to do.

A crowd of banner-carrying pickets stood

around the gates of the hospital. They were a fairly good-natured bunch, being watched over by a tolerant London policeman making sure that there was room for people to pass. Among them were porters, orderlies and domestics and some nurses whom Anne knew. A few greeted her as she walked by them in jeans and sweatshirt, her uniform in her holdall.

One loud-mouthed, scruffy-looking man called after her, 'Scab!'

She stopped abruptly and turned back to face him. 'Talking to me?' she asked icily.

'Yeah!' he leered. 'Why don't you come and join us?'

'Listen, you,' she returned in a cutting tone, 'suppose you were taken desperately ill and the doctors were on strike. What then?'

He brazened it out. 'Well, they wouldn't be, would they? It's against their rules.'

'What do you care about rules?' she exploded. 'And I don't know you. I don't think you're even from this hospital. Go to hell!'

Her anger had abated somewhat by the time she had reached the staff-room and put on her uniform before going to the ward. Reporting her experience to Don, who was duty charge nurse that day, she said, 'Some people think strikes are the only way to achieve anything, but it seems to me it's just union officials stirring up trouble to boost their own self-importance.'

Don laughed. 'OK, Annie, let them get on with it. We've got more important things to do.'

'Ready, willing and able,' she returned cheerfully. 'What can I do?' She was quite prepared to do anything at all, since there were no porters to deliver patients to wherever, no messengers to collect samples for the path lab, no one to bring fresh laundry, no one to lay up lunch trays or fetch food from the kitchens, no one to damp dust or clean the floors. Instead she found herself being given the responsibility of a new patient.

Anne learned that the neurosurgeons had been working half the night on the victim of a shooting incident.

'He's Edward Jones, aged fifty,' Don explained. 'A night watchman . . . got shot in the head when he surprised this gang trying to rob the store where he worked.'

'Oh, poor man!' Anne sympathised. 'How is he?'

Don turned down the corners of his mouth. 'Touch and go. They had to do a craniotomy to remove bone fragments and blood clots along the path of the bullet. It went in at the right temporal lobe and out of the right occipital. He's had all the medication they can give him. Even if he makes it, he's lost a bit of his brain. Might be better if he didn't. Anyway, I want you to special him. I had to put Shirley in there for the time being, but she's none too confident.'

Anne made an anxious face. 'This'll be my first experience of a gunshot wound.'

'Well, he just needs the same attention as any other deeply unconscious patient. The usual neuro obs, two-hourly turning, mouth care, eye care, fluid charting. Professor Drapper's in the doctor's office, talking to Mrs Jones. Grant and Bob are still with the patient. Come on, I'll take you along.'

Anne went with Don to meet her new responsibility. Grant was there, painstakingly checking the equipment surrounding the gravely injured man, while the timid new staff nurse looked on with big anxious eyes.

'All right, Shirley,' the charge nurse said, 'Anne will take over now. You go and have your lunch.'

Anne's heart filled with compassion for the big man lying prostrate in the bed. His breathing was being assisted by a ventilator, he was linked to a heart monitor, and a cerebral function monitor, and a blood transfusion. A man with a bandaged head whose life hung by a thread. An ordinary man who this time yesterday had been able-bodied, going about his own affairs. He could have been anybody's dad.

Bob gave Anne a hopeless shrug,

Grant looked up from checking the cerebral function monitor. 'We've just given him Mannitol. Let me know of any change in the ICP, Anne,' he said. 'And his wife can come in now, Don, for a short while.' The registrar's concerned gaze returned to his patient. 'I hope the Professor has prepared her properly . . . Encourage her not to stay too long.'

Anne nodded, and swallowed, and set about making her own checks of the equipment when the doctors left. Then she tidied the bedclothes and gently sponged a trace of dried blood from the face of the victim, so as not to distress his wife any more than could be helped.

The woman, when the charge nurse brought her along, moved like someone in a trance. 'I'll send in some tea,' murmured Don.

She was a small person with a good figure for her age and modern-styled short brown hair. Her eyes were stark with shock in her chalk-white face. But she didn't cry. Her first reaction seemed like total disbelief that this was happening to her. Then it was anger as the truth could not be denied. 'B-bloody thugs!' she muttered, her hands going to her face. 'Bloody . . . bloody . . . bloody . . .' And then the tears came. 'Oh, God!' she sobbed. 'He can't hear me, can he? Ted hates me swearing.'

Anne put her arms around the distraught woman, saying gently, 'He'd understand . . . he'd probably agree with you this time. Come and sit down, love.'

She pulled out a chair and they sat together talking quietly while the wife held her husband's limp hand. 'You're so kind, all of you,' she said brokenly.

Anne shook her head. 'I only wish there was more we could do. Look, sorry I have to be here, but you talk to him. Although he's unconscious, he may be hearing.'

Hazel came to relieve her for her afternoon break, and when she returned Mrs Jones had gone away for a time.

'Said she'd be back this evening,' Hazel reported. They went through the motions of washing and turning the inert body which was Ted Jones, putting his prescribed medication into the IV tube. 'Looks as if she'd better hurry,' Hazel added, her lips pursing.

'I think you're right,' Anne sighed. She felt increasing heaviness, as though all the weight of the world's wickedness rested on her slim shoulders.

They saw a lot of Grant that afternoon, popping in and out at intervals. He arrived for the fourth time, in answer to Anne's report about a significant rise in cerebral pressure, and at that precise moment she was viewing the heart monitor with alarm. Quite suddenly an uncoordinated chaotic tracing had appeared. It was followed by the long flat trace and whine which heralded failure.

The registrar sprang into action, whipping back the bedclothes and giving a mighty cardiac thump. 'Get the crash team,' he yelled to Anne. 'Give me the paddles . . . come *on* . . . move, girl!'

She responded swiftly to his order by pulling the emergency buzzer, but she was shocked beyond belief. She had felt sad but relieved that her patient had died so peacefully. Her hands were trembling as she lubricated the defibrillator paddles before handing them over. 'I don't agree with this,' she said. 'Let him go.'

By now other staff had come running. Anne looked on grimly as the anaesthetist gave adrenalin and Grant tried to shock the silenced heart into action.

All their efforts were in vain. Ted Jones had gone

to his Maker.

'Well, we tried,' Grant said wearily.

'That was positively indecent. Why?' Anne snapped.

'Don't be stupid, girl,' Grant snapped back. 'I'm here to try to save life, aren't I?'

'What kind of life? A half-paralysed cabbage, dependent on other people for the rest of his days? I'm glad you failed.' She ran away to the staff-room and wept.

Presently Hazel came to find her, bringing a coffee. 'Grant told me to come,' she said. 'Don't get upset, Annie. We can't win 'em all.'

'I'm all right,' Anne sniffed and blew her nose. 'I just feel so bloody useless, that's the trouble.'

At nine-thirty Anne was heartily glad to be going off duty. By this time Ted Jones lay undisturbed in the chapel of rest and distressing meetings with his family were over. Grant had been writing up notes in his office. He joined her when she left.

'Are we on speaking terms again?' he asked quietly, accompanying her to the lift.

'We were never otherwise,' she said, 'although I still think you were wrong.'

'Let's not hold any inquests.' There were other people in the lift and no more was said until they alighted. 'Are you going back to your flat?' he asked, looking at her solicitously, his dark head on one side.

'Yes. Goodnight,' she returned, about to make for the main gates.

But he put an arm around her waist and steered

her in the direction of the doctors' car park. 'I know a nice transport caff where we can have fish and chips and you can tell me all your troubles. How about that?'

Anne smiled wanly, melting at his touch. *'You're* my trouble,' she said.

'Me?' His deep voice went up an octave. 'I'm the most amenable guy that ever was!'

Already she felt a little better. 'Professor Higgins Mark Two,' she said drily.

He opened the door of his car to let her in. 'Professor who?'

'Don't tell me you've never seen *My Fair Lady?*'

'Oh, *that* dumbo,' Grant said cheerfully, making his way out of the car park. 'Couldn't see what was staring him in the face, could he?'

'No . . . there are people like that,' Anne agreed.

It wasn't a transport caff, as he put it. It was a very nice fish restaurant near Camden Passage, with homely red-check tablecloths and candles in old wine bottles, and a jovial Austrian proprietor.

'Not quite Chatswood Gardens style, but the grub's terrific,' Grant assured her.

They had plaice and chips followed by home-made *apfelstrudel* with cream. Anne hadn't thought she could face food, but she discovered she was really hungry.

'That was delicious,' she said, finishing her pudding. 'How did you find this place?'

'Oh, I've been around. I know a lot of low dives.'

She smiled. 'Don't let the proprietor hear you say that! He's every right to be proud of himself.'

Grant broke a runlet of wax from the side of the red candle. 'I'm not all that proud of me,' he admitted, screwing it into a ball. 'I'm sorry you were upset today, but it isn't easy making spot decisions. I reacted as you might expect to a flat trace.'

'I know,' she said, 'it's your training. Let's talk about something else.'

He brightened. 'Right. How about if I told you I made your sister happy today?'

Anne's eyes widened. 'You did? How was that?'

'Professor Drapper was extremely interested when I put the idea of the TV programme to him. He'd be glad of a chance to give his views. He suggested Michelle gets in touch with his secretary at his Harley Street rooms, to fix an appointment, and I passed on the message.'

'Oh, great. Thanks, Grant. That was good of you.'

The registrar waved a careless hand. 'What else could I do after the lavish party she put on for us?' He eyed Anne thoughtfully. 'You're so different, you two girls.'

'In looks, you mean?'

'Not just that. I should imagine your sister goes through life like a force-nine gale . . . whereas you, give or take the odd tantrum, are as calm as a zephyr breeze.'

'Oh, dear, am I that dull?' Anne returned.

He didn't reply, but his eyes meeting hers over the candlelit table, held quite a different meaning, one which forced her to drop her gaze as her senses reacted urgently to unspoken messages.

She was glad of the diversion when a waitress brought them coffee, with little plastic pots of cream in the saucers. Pulling back the foil on her portion, she dribbled the cream into her cup and stirred. 'I get worried about Mich sometimes,' she told him. 'She's a high-flyer . . . feels she has to prove herself. That producer's a forceful character, isn't he? I didn't altogether care for Joe.'

'Mmm, he could be overpowering,' Grant reflected. 'But why are you worried? Michelle seemed full of confidence to me.'

'Oh, that's an act. I found out she's been turning to tranquillisers to help her performance.' Anne hesitated. 'She's on Diazepam. It was prescribed for migraine.'

He was too captivated by the limpid beauty of her lovely green eyes to give his full attention to Michelle's problems. 'I expect what she really needs is a man,' he joked.

Anne rolled her eyes in exasperation. 'For heaven's sake!' she exclaimed. 'If your foot was handy, I'd stamp on it! It was a man who shattered her life in the first place.'

The registrar brought himself back to the facts. 'Oh, yes, of course . . . her divorce. His fault, was it?'

'Yes, very much so. They hadn't been married long when it turned out he was bisexual, which was something of a bombshell.'

He nodded. 'Yes, it would be,' he agreed.

'Anyway, I've tried to warn her off the pills, but

she's inclined to blow her top when I do.' Anne sighed and lifted back the fall of her blonde hair. 'Any suggestions? I mean, seriously, Grant.'

His chiselled features settled into thoughtful lines. 'And she gets this drug for migraine, you say. You don't really think she's dependent?'

'No . . . but I want to stop it coming to that.'

'There was a piece in *The Lancet* recently,' he remembered, 'about a new drug for migraine at present undergoing tests, but there's no wonder cure so far. In any case, stress is an important factor. She should try to relax, slow down a bit. Controlled breathing can help, and taking account of any foods which trigger off an attack.'

'A lot easier said than done,' Anne remarked. 'She has to do a lot of wining and dining in that job.'

'Hmm. Alcohol is *not* a good idea in association with pills. Perhaps she does need some counselling . . . or something good to happen in her life.' His blue eyes gleamed, as though he had just thought of something. 'I wonder if we could make it happen?'

'How do you mean?' she asked.

'Well, I know that Brad has leanings in her direction. He's also making a special study of migraine. Does she like him?'

Anne smiled. 'I think she does. They got on very well together the other night.'

'Fine. He mentioned that he'd like to see her again. I'll encourage him to go ahead, and while he's about it he could do her a good turn with some tactful advice. She might take it better from him. Nothing like a bit of light romance for lifting the spirits,' Grant declared blithely.

'Do what you like, with my blessing,' Anne said, laughing. 'Michelle will decide if that's what she wants. She can be jolly stubborn when it suits her.'

Grant restrained a smile. 'Now that's something you do both have in common.' He drained his cup. 'You ready? Right, let's go.'

He settled the modest bill and they went out into the seedy High Street to walk the short distance to where they had left the car. It took barely ten minutes to drive to Anne's flat. They talked little on the journey, but it was a companionable silence. Now Anne didn't know quite what to expect as, switching off the engine, he turned to look at her. It was eleven-thirty and they'd already had coffee. She had no intention of suggesting some more and being turned down.

'Well, here we are again,' said Grant, his eyes creasing at the corners.

'Yes, and thank you very much for feeding me. I needed that.' Her inside was twisting itself into knots. In a moment would he take her in his arms and kiss her in that half tender, inflaming fashion which had nearly driven her mad last time? She thought she ought to be less responsive tonight—if she could manage it. He was too sure of himself.

Beyond putting his arm along the back of her seat, however, Grant made no move towards her straight away. 'So you didn't mind slumming tonight?'

'Slumming?' Anne gave a puzzled smile. 'Mandy and I often have fish and chips, and our chippy's not as upmarket as yours. That was a funny sort of remark.'

'Yes, it was. Forget it.' He gave a short laugh. 'We all say stupid things sometimes. It was a very pleasant finish to a rather awful day, wasn't it?'

The demise of Ted Jones was still uppermost in Anne's memory. 'Don't remind me! Many more days like that, and I don't know whether I can take it.' She had to catch her bottom lip between her teeth to control the tremble.

Grant laid his hand on her shoulder. 'Now, now,' he said with mock severity, 'enough of that defeatist talk. Remember, we count the success rate, not the failures. There's Michael back on his feet and getting all his parts working properly . . . there's Alistair Carle home and following the horses again, I shouldn't wonder. Two out of three's not bad going, is it?'

Looking into the strong, sympathetic face so close to hers, she managed a smile. 'When you put it like that, I suppose not.'

He tutted and shook his head. 'Dear me! I thought they'd picked well when they chose you. What can I suggest to take your mind off things? Hot chocolate . . . a good book before you go to sleep?'

Anne pretended a yawn. 'I shan't need anything tonight . . . not even a goodnight kiss!' she added with a touch of her usual impudence.

He threw back his head and laughed. 'Was that

an invitation?'

'It certainly wasn't!'

'Well, *you* may be all right, Anne . . . but what about me? Doctors have their bad times too, you know. I could do with a little something to lift my spirits.'

His lips were seductively close—so near that she couldn't resist bridging the gap between them. She had meant it to be just a brief, teasing brush of her lips, finishing with some flippant rejoinder before they parted. But the kiss lingered on, the moist warm contact too breathtaking for sanity. It was sweet, fulfilling, demanding, and as heady as champagne.

'I must go, I must go,' Anne murmured weakly, as his ardent mouth left hers and travelled to her throat.

'Must you?' he returned huskily, his arms drawing her closer instead of relaxing their hold.

With an effort she gathered the last of her will-power and pushed away. 'Please, Grant, please . . . I ought to go.'

He loosed her reluctantly then, sitting back in his own seat, smoothing a hand over his hair, his face grim. 'Yes, you're right . . . that was going farther than I intended.' His manner became almost hostile, as though she had in some way inveigled him into action he regretted. 'Off you go, then,' he ordered brusquely.

Anne ran indoors in a state of unhappy confusion. Oh, yes, undoubtedly he found her physically attractive. But was that all it had meant to him tonight . . . a casual flirtation? Surely there must have been more to it than that? You could feel when a thing was right for both of you. Why then had he been short with her when she had called a halt? He should have understood and been glad that she wasn't an easy push-over. Although there was a certain chemistry between them, there was also a kind of barrier, and she didn't know what to do about it.

St Martin's Hospital weathered the second day of the strike and then things returned to normal. Nobody seemed to know what, if anything, had been achieved, but there were vague promises that privatisation of cleaning services and other grievances would be reviewed.

Anne was able to take her postponed days off and she met her sister for lunch during one of them. She was intrigued to find out what had come of the registrar's suggestions, not having had an opportunity for a private talk with him since that disturbing Monday evening. It didn't really surprise her to discover that he had kept his word about Michelle.

Her sister was in radiant form over their salad lunch at Selfridges. 'I must hand it to Grant,' she enthused. 'He got cracking and I'm seeing Professor Drapper at his rooms on Friday morning. Joe was impressed with his status. Did you know he's a member of the World Health Organisation?'

'No,' said Anne, 'but I thought he'd be a good choice.'

Michelle bubbled on. 'Guess who I'm spending the day with on Sunday?'

'Go on, surprise me,' Anne said, breaking open her crusty roll.

'Bradley. He wants to repay me for my dinner party because he enjoyed it so much. He *is* rather sweet, isn't he? So I thought I'd show him Blenheim Palace, since he's really into English heritage. Then we can wine and dine somewhere along the river . . .'

'Don't forget he's a struggling doctor, will you?' Anne warned, laughing.

'Oh, Brad's not short of a dollar or two,' Michelle returned. 'He's a Harvard man. And his father's in banking, I do know that.'

Anne chuckled. 'It doesn't take you long to dig things out! Well, *vive* international goodwill, as they say. And don't do anything I wouldn't do.'

'By the way,' Michelle cut in, 'Daddy reminded me about his charity ball at the Café Royal in two weeks' time.'

'Oh, gosh! I'd forgotten about that,' Anne said.

'I'd got it in my diary. He wants to know who we're bringing, for the table plans. He's taking Aunt Laura. I thought, if it goes all right with Brad on Sunday, I'd ask him. And you could ask Grant, unless you've someone else in mind?'

'We-ell . . .' Anne hesitated, her heart slipping a beat, 'I don't know how I stand with Grant . . . he puzzles me sometimes. But I suppose, if you're asking Brad, then that would be different. When will you let me know if you are?'

'Oh, take it as definite, then, as time's getting short,' Michelle said airily, 'or they may make other plans.'

They said goodbye after a pleasant interlude shopping in the West End. Anne had been pleased at the fresh bounciness in her sister's manner. Maybe Grant was right, she mused, a new romantic interest might be just what Michelle needed.

Ringing Devon that evening to find out how Mandy's injured foot was progressing, Anne found her flatmate also amazingly cheerful.

'Annie, I'm in love!' she confided in a dreamy voice. 'It's going to be the real thing, I'm convinced.'

'Oh? This is all a bit sudden, isn't it?' Anne teased. 'I thought you were supposed to be grounded. Where did you find this Prince Charming?'

'He picked me up off the beach when I cut my foot. Carried me all the way to his car and took me to the hospital . . . and never mind the blood all over his nice white trousers! I've seen him practically every day since. He's a local man,' Mandy went on, 'teaches science at the grammar school here. *And* my dad approves.'

'Well, your dad did tell me that out of adversity cometh blessing.' Anne laughed. 'Romance seems to be in the air at the moment.' She told her friend all that had transpired since meeting Brad and Grant at Covent Garden market that day. 'Brad's really the first man Michelle's been interested in since her divorce.'

'And does that go for you and Grant as well?' Mandy asked curiously.

'Good heavens, no! One step forward, two steps backwards with us. Although I must admit, I'm rather smitten,' Anne sighed. 'Anyway, I'm keeping my feet on the ground for the time being. It's safer there.'

Putting down the phone, she sighed again. It was all very well for Grant to prescribe romance as a remedy for tension. That was OK if you could treat it as fun. But when you were in danger of losing your heart to someone who didn't give a hoot for you, then that wasn't remedial. That was disaster.

CHAPTER SEVEN

THE POSTPONED rounders match between Fleming and Jenner wards took place on Saturday afternoon, in the playing field behind the residents' quarters.

Coming off duty at four-thirty that day, Anne hurried along with some of the other nurses to catch the closing stages of the match. There was much ragging and catcalling as the rival spectators supported their teams.

'Go, go, go, Don!' yelled Anne, jumping up and down with the rest as their charge nurse raced to complete the final circuit and win Fleming the match.

'So why weren't you playing?' asked a rich deep voice behind her.

With a lurch of her heart she turned to find Grant there. She had been scanning the crowd for him, hoping there might be a chance afterwards to speak about the charity ball, but she hadn't seen him anywhere.

'Hi!' she said brightly, determined to act as though whatever had happened between them was of little importance. 'I was working. What's your excuse?'

'Had to get my car MOT'd. And do some essential shopping.'

Some people had begun to make tracks for the medical staff mess-room. Others stood around in small groups, chatting in the late afternoon sunshine. But Anne was lost in the fascinating depths of Grant's arresting blue eyes. She hardly took in his reply, until Georges Alain joined them and put an arm around her shoulders.

'What 'e needs, Anne,' said Georges, 'is a wife to do 'is shopping for 'im. Coming for a drink, you two?'

'Yes, why not?' said Grant. 'Thirsty work, cheering.'

'A fat lot of cheering you did,' Anne scoffed while the three of them sauntered back to the common-room. 'You didn't arrive until it was over.'

Grant gave a wry smile. 'Because you didn't see me it doesn't mean I hadn't got you in my sights.'

Georges looked from one to the other and stroked his dark beard thoughtfully as they made for the bar.

Meanwhile the ritual presentation of a 'trophy' was going on. Don climbed on to a chair to wave the plastic model of a shrunken head which Dr Arbuthnot had brought back from abroad. There were calls for a re-match and a great deal of ribaldry. Someone put a cassette in the music centre, adding to the general clamour, and before long the room was filled with dancing feet.

It set Anne's own tapping. She put her glass down on a table and swivelled her hips with attractive grace to the strong beat of the music. 'Come on, you guys,' she urged. 'Loosen up!'

Grant was evidently not in dancing mood, but Georges, who had been watching her with frank admiration, was happy to join in. They twisted and jived together until Anne collapsed laughing on to a seat, fanning herself with her hand.

The anaesthetist flopped beside her, mopping his brow. 'I grow too old for zis. You would like another drink?'

'Yes, please, Georges. Just an orange juice.'

He glanced towards the bar where Grant stood with a brooding expression, staring in their direction. 'What is the matter wiz my friend over there?' murmured Georges. 'You 'ave been upsetting 'im?'

'Me?' She laughed innocently. 'I don't upset people . . . and I'm the last person to know what goes on inside *his* head!'

After levelling a long questioning look at her from beneath his dark brows, Georges kissed her on the nose. 'You also are very wicked, little one. Come . . . let us go and cheer 'im up.'

Taking her hand, he tugged her back to where the registrar was, bought her the drink and after a few commonplace remarks, left them together.

'Used up all your surplus energy?' Grant asked with a restrained smile.

'For the time being. I love dancing. I find it much more therapeutic than *your* remedy for stress,' Anne replied merrily.

'Oh, you do, do you?' He studied her with a critical candour which set her blood pulsating. 'Well, we each have to find our own solution for that in the end.'

'True!' She sipped her juice. Actually she was rather glad that Georges had taken himself off somewhere, since it gave her the opportunity to tell Grant about the charity ball. Now was as good a time as any, although she felt ridiculously nervous and not at all sure what his reaction would be. Hesitating, she took another drink before making the attempt. 'There was something I wanted to ask you, Grant.'

He inclined his dark head in a listening fashion. 'Yes?'

She drew a long breath, choosing her words carefully. 'Well, first, thanks for fixing things for Michelle . . . she was really happy when I saw her last.'

'OK, fine. Was that it?'

'No,' she laughed, 'that's just the beginning. I . . .'

'Look, it's too noisy in here,' he interrupted. 'Why don't we go outside if you want to talk?'

Anne nodded and allowed herself to be led on to the veranda where there were a number of benches at intervals along the length of the building.

'Now,' he said, sitting beside her, and with the kind of disarming smile he might give to a nervous patient, 'what's on your mind?'

With his entire attention focused on her, Anne felt even more diffident about having to approach him. She plunged in by repeating her thanks on Michelle's behalf. 'I don't know whether you're in the picture,' she went on, 'but she's spending the *whole day* with Brad tomorrow.'

'Yes, I had heard. You're pleased about that, are you?'

'Mmm, I think so. She also intends to invite him

to a charity ball my father is involved with. I—er—I mean, we . . . thought it might be a nice idea if I asked you, to make up the table.'

There, it was said. And she knew her colour was rising and she wished she could vanish into a hole in the ground. 'What do you think? Of course, you may be booked up already,' she added, wanting to give him an exit-line. 'Don't worry if you can't make it. I can easily find someone else.'

'Hold it!' Grant controlled the smile escaping the corners of his mouth. 'I'm sure you could. But unless I know when and where this bash is to be held, how can I tell you?'

Anne laughed. 'Oh, sorry, didn't I say? It's a fortnight today . . . at the Café Royal. Not very long notice, I'm afraid.'

He pursed his lips, considering. 'Sounds OK. Yes, I'd like to come, although I'll have to confirm that. Will it be a grand occasion?'

'Yes, it will be quite dressy,' said Anne. She was relieved and happy. Somehow she hadn't expected such a spontaneous acceptance. 'We thought it would be another nice experience for Brad,' she continued by way of explanation.

Grant gave a sardonic grin. 'I don't know what it is about this fellow that merits so much attention from the Westlake sisters. By the way what charity is the ball in aid of?'

'It will cover a number, I expect. My father is a City Alderman. His livery company supports hospitals and schools and so forth.'

'Oh, I see.' Grant digested this information

without further comment. After a reflective pause he went on, 'Tell me . . . are you doing anything tomorrow?'

She looked at him in surprise. 'Well, I'm working in the morning, but after that, nothing special.'

'Like to come with me to a birthday party?'

It was just a careless, off-the-cuff invitation, such as often happened in their wide circle, but a small seed of joy quickened inside her. He wouldn't have asked her if he didn't feel something for her, would he? 'Yes, I'd love to,' she said. 'Whose birthday . . . and where?'

'A lady I'm fond of . . . in the East End of London.'

'Not the one you told me about—the one who's condemned you to a lonely old age?' Anne queried with a half-smile.

His lips puckered, as he recalled their former exchange. 'No, not that one. I don't even know when *her* birthday is. This is my foster-mother. She's sixty tomorrow.'

Anne's mouth gaped a little. 'Your foster-mother? I didn't know . . .'

'Well, of course you didn't,' Grant cut in gruffly. 'You know damn all about me.' He glanced at his wristwatch. 'Look, I must dash. Pick you up at your place tomorrow around four-thirty. All right?' They both stood up as he prepared to leave.

'What shall I wear?' she asked.

'Oh, just an ordinary dress. This won't be a posh do.' He sketched her a brief goodbye and was gone.

Anne stood for a moment transfixed and

wondering at his disclosure. Not that it was anything extraordinary for people to have foster-mothers. It was just that she had never thought about who or where his family might be. And not that it mattered very much either, unless there was some dark and dreadful disaster connected with them. Well, it was no good letting her imagination run riot. Having mentioned it, he would probably explain in due course.

Going back into the residents' mess where dancing was still in full swing, Anne was joined again by Georges.

'You 'ave sorted your troubles?' he asked.

She laughed. 'What troubles, Georges? I don't have any.'

He laid a finger alongside his nose. 'Love is full of troubles, no?'

'Georges, you're a romantic chump,' Anne returned, 'but I wish Englishmen were as easy to understand.' She rolled her eyes in mock despair and then grinned. 'I'm going out with him tomorrow. Does that satisfy you?'

The Frenchman nodded and wagged a finger at her. 'Be nice to 'im. 'E is a good guy.'

'He's a pain!' she retorted.

Anne was glad to be working that Sunday morning or she would have gone crazy with waiting for four-thirty to arrive. Things were pleasantly busy in Fleming Ward and Don gave her the care of their new patient, Harold Wells, admitted overnight from Casualty. He was a seventy-year-old heavyweight who had fallen on the stone staircase leading from his flat, sustaining a gash on the head and severe bruising. The night staff reported that he was complaining of headache.

'Not surprising, is it? said Don. 'Get him sitting out for breakfast and he can go back again when his bed's made.'

Anne went to make herself known to the elderly balding man reclining on pillows. There was a dressing over the stitched wound in his left temporal region and grazes down that side of his lined face.

'Good morning, Mr Wells,' Anne said. 'My goodness, you *have* been in the wars!'

'Hello, love,' he wheezed. 'Yes, tripped over my own feet, didn't I? Easy done. Don't know why they stuck me in here just for this, though.'

Anne smiled. 'Well, you knocked yourself out for a few minutes, didn't you? We can't afford to take risks with our senior citizens. Got to make sure you're steady on your pins before we release you. Let's get you sitting out for breakfast—that's a start.'

She found his dressing-gown, steadied him while he put it on, and helped him to a chair. 'You sound a little chesty.'

He nodded. 'Always been a bit bronchial. Too much weight, that's my trouble. Not that I'm very hungry this morning.' He put a gnarled hand to his head.

'It aches, does it?' she sympathised. 'You'll be getting something for that soon, and you can go back to bed when it's made. I'll come and have a talk with you later. Then you can tell me all about yourself.'

There were no startling happenings and no doctors' rounds to upset routine. Bedbound patients were washed and cared for, treatments given and drugs dispensed, and after her coffee-break Anne had time to sit with Harold Wells and take his history.

It was not an uncommon story in that part of London. He was living alone since his wife died, and in a high-rise block of flats where the lifts were constantly out of commission. 'It's no fun trailing up and down all them steps to the fifth floor,' he said. 'My daughter helps with the shopping when she can, but she's got her own family to see to.'

Taking his pulse and blood-pressure, Anne found the pulse sluggish and blood-pressure on the high side. 'Have you enquired if there's anything better, perhaps in sheltered accommodation?' she asked.

'No, love, I haven't bothered. There's bound to be a waiting list long as you arm.'

She smiled. 'Perhaps our medical social worker could put in a word. We'll get her to come and see you.'

She reported all her findings to Don, who promised to contact the social worker, although he wasn't very optimistic. 'Still, if you don't ask, you won't get,' he agreed.

Anne went off duty at one, feeling she had at least started the ball rolling to find Mr Wells better accommodation.

On the way back to her flat she stopped to buy a box of luxury soaps as a token birthday gift for Grant's foster-mother. She imagined *he* might buy her flowers, and not everybody liked chocolates, so toiletries seemed the best choice.

Dressed as he had suggested, in a simple floral shirtwaister, and with her blonde hair combed free, she was ready when Grant sounded his horn on drawing up outside. Picking up her white linen jacket, shoulder bag and the gift, Anne went out to meet him, eager as a teenager on her first date.

'Will I do?' she asked with a warm smile, and giving a twirl.

Standing back, hands in the pockets of his stylish sports trousers, he raised his dark eyebrows in approval. 'Fresh as a daisy and twice as beautiful,' he said, and opened the car door for her. 'Ruth will be impressed.'

'Ruth being your foster-mother?' she queried when they were en route.

'Yes. I used to call her Auntie Ruth as a child—we all did.'

Anne waited, admiring his strong, handsome profile as he concentrated on the road, driving eastwards. 'We *all* did?' she repeated when he remained silent. 'Are you going to tell me about it . . . or should I mind my own business?'

Pausing at traffic lights, he cast her a sideways glance and laughed. 'What a diplomat you are! Since I'm taking you to meet the lady who gave me a home when I needed one, you may as well know the why and wherefore.'

The lights changed to green and they drove on past the Sunday market crowds at Petticoat Lane before he continued. 'My own mother was killed by a hit-and-run driver when I was six. My father looked after me then. We were doing fine, until three years later. He decided to paint the eaves of the house, fell off the top of the ladder and died as a result.'

'Oh, dear, how dreadful!' exclaimed Anne, shocked as she pictured the plight of one small boy with his world in ruins. 'Wasn't there . . . anyone else to look after you?'

'No. My mother and father were both only children. He was an office worker and only just making both ends meet, so there was little money. I was taken into care and ended up with Ruth. She couldn't have been more caring if she'd been my own mother. But for her, who knows what would have become of me?'

'Well, that's certainly a wonderful tribute, Grant,' Anne said softly. 'She must be very proud of what you've achieved. Does she have a family of her own?'

'No, although she was married. Her husband was a nice guy—a postman—dead now. There've been lots of children through her hands. Some'll be there today, I expect.' He was silent for a moment, then he said, 'Now you know my beginnings. Very different from your sheltered childhood, I imagine.'

Anne shrugged. 'We can't choose where we're born or what happens to us. My life has had its ups and downs, but nothing quite as devastating as yours.'

'Yes, I know your own mother died tragically,' Grant said. 'It was having gone through a similar experience which made me empathise with you the other day.'

They were approaching East Ham and he turned down a long side-road lined with red-leaved prunus trees. The houses were old but substantially built. Some were down-at-heel, others smart with new window frames and colourful doors. Grant drew to a halt outside one in good repair. A bunch of balloons fluttered gaily from the laurel bush in the modest front garden.

'This is it. Come and meet my only family,' he said.

When he knocked, the door was opened by a large, round-faced woman who flung her arms wide to give the doctor the biggest, most exuberant hug and kiss Anne had ever seen.

'Hello, my love! Oh, it's so nice of you to come,' she exclaimed. 'And what about all those gorgeous flowers you sent? You shouldn't be so extravagant, really you shouldn't.'

'They were all right, were they?' Grant smiled. 'Thought I'd better send them, just in case I couldn't make it. Ruth, this is Anne, one of our nurses from the hospital.'

'Hello, Ruth. I've been hearing all about you,' Anne said. 'Happy birthday!' and she handed over the small package.

'For me? Oh, thank you, dear. I am being spoiled

today,' Ruth beamed. 'Come along in, both of you, and meet everyone.'

A small dark-eyed coloured boy came from the living-room from where a considerable amount of noise was coming. Thumb in mouth, he stopped and fixed the strangers with a solemn stare.

'Hello! Who have we here?' asked Grant with a smile.

'This is Simmy,' Ruth explained. 'He's come to stay with me until his mummy's better, haven't you, pet?' Aside, she murmured, 'Got beaten up by her boyfriend, poor soul.'

'When are you going to retire?' laughed Grant.

'Aw, what would I do if I retired?' Ruth retorted. 'Just grow older and fatter. The kids keep me young.'

It was a birthday party like no other Anne had ever been to. Ruth was caring for three children at that time—Simeon, and a brother and sister aged three and five. In the homely living-room there was also a crowd of visitors of various sizes and persuasions, and greetings cards were two and three deep on mantelpiece and windowsill.

They all seemed at home and enjoying themselves, even the most successful of Ruth's erstwhile charges, Grant Ryder, neurosurgeon, who eventually sat on the floor to make a model out of Lego for little Simeon.

'The doctor was always a gifted child,' Ruth confided to Anne. 'Won his way to the top with scholarships. He went to public school as well as university, you know. And he never forgot me—always came to see me in the holidays.'

'I know he thinks you're a very special person,' Anne told her.

As she watched the lively company, one thing was clear to her. It was the radiant goodness which shone from this rather plain, childless woman that had warmed all her substitute children. She had truly found her niche in life. She loved freely and without reserve.

'Are you and him . . . walking out? Ruth asked carefully.

'I wouldn't say that,' Anne smiled. 'So far we're just good friends.'

The other woman nodded. 'Oh, well, excuse me being nosey, but I'd like to see him settled with a nice wife, you see.'

'Keep your fingers crossed, then,' laughed Anne.

Grant, having finished his model-making, joined them in time to overhear her remark. 'This girl's in a perpetual state of crossed fingers,' he joked. 'What's it in aid of this time?'

'Never you mind,' his foster-mother returned. 'That was women's talk.'

After the cutting of the birthday cake and the singing of the birthday song, Grant and Anne said their goodbyes.

It was seven-thirty and a pleasant summer evening. 'Do you want to go back to town? Or shall we take a run out to Buckhurst Hill and a pub I know?' Grant suggested.

'That sounds great. I don't know much about this side of the river.' Anne belted herself in and they set off.

'You're very thoughtful,' he remarked some ten minutes later. 'What's the matter? Did my modest beginnings shock you?'

'Surprised me, would be more to the point,' she admitted. 'I'm amazed that anyone could have got as far as you have without resources. It must have been tough going.'

'I was helped,' he said. 'My public school fees were taken care of by a charitable trust, like the kind your father supports. And it's amazing what you can earn during vacations, if you don't mind what you do.' He smiled reflectively. 'I've been waiter, barman, fruit-picker. Good fun on the whole, and I met some smashing people.'

'It was certainly a lucky break that you landed with Ruth,' Anne said. 'What a lovely lady! I'm glad I came.' She paused. 'Why did you ask me to come, Grant?'

He shrugged. 'Perhaps I wanted you to see how the other half lives.'

She looked at him sharply. 'And what does that mean? I don't exactly go around with my eyes shut.'

It was evidently not a subject he was prepared to discuss at that moment. They happened to be passing open common land, some of it marked out as football pitches. 'This is Wanstead Flats,' he told her. 'I've kicked a ball around here a few times, along with other East End kids.'

Anne surveyed the dreary expanse without comment, knowing instinctively that some important issue was at stake, but confused as to what.

The miles were passing quickly. They travelled through sprawling residential areas with patches of grassland between, coming at last to the green borders of Epping Forest. Hawthorn was heavy with bloom, horse-chestnut trees were awash with pink and white candles, and the evening air was sweetly scented.

Driving into a sleepy hollow near an old country inn, Grant brought the car to a standstill. 'Shall we walk first?' he said.

'Mmm, that would be nice,' she agreed.

He knew his way about. They mounted a rise and skirted a cricket field fringed with buttercups. 'Scored a few runs on this ground,' he told her.

The turf was springy beneath their feet and the birds had begun their evensong. Although traffic rushed by on the road below, a peace pervaded the Sunday evening countryside. 'It's really lovely here,' said Anne, enjoying the view.

They spoke little as they strolled on. Both were wrapped in their own thoughts. Anne was happy to be with Grant but oddly disturbed by a kind of distance in his manner. He didn't even take her hand.

All at once she limped and winced. 'Ouch! Something pricking my foot.' Sitting on a nearby felled tree trunk, she took off her open-toed sandal and shook out a spiky piece of twig that had crept inside.

He came to sit alongside her on the time-worn trunk carved with lovers' initials, watching while she brushed the debris from her foot and shook the sandal before putting it back on.

'That's better. Not really the right footwear for country walks,' she smiled. 'I'd have brought some flatties if I'd known what you had in mind.'

'I didn't know what I had in mind,' he said, picking up a grey ring-dove's feather lying on the grass and smoothing it between his fingers. 'In fact, I've never been so indecisive in my whole life as I've been lately.'

She glanced at his strong capable hands stroking the feather. 'Oh, well, we all go through periods like that. Here, let me plant that for good luck.' Reaching over, she took his feather and stuck the quill into the ground.

'For luck?' Grant's mouth twisted satirically. 'That's a new one on me. But I suppose you learn different folklore in the nurseries of Kensington.'

'You *are* in a mood tonight. What's biting you?' she challenged.

Turning to face her, he met her troubled green eyes squarely. 'You're not going to like what I have to say, Anne.'

Her manner lightened. 'You can't make the charity ball . . . is that it?'

'No, not that. I'll come to your ball. But I want to make it plain from the outset how we stand.'

'What are you driving at?' she returned, wide-eyed, her stomach lurching.

'Look, let's be honest about this . . .' He scratched his head with a kind of despair. 'I know and *you* know that we're . . . well, mutually attracted, for want of a better description. But I have to spell it out . . . there's no future in it.'

A shiver crept over her skin. She felt hot and cold at the same time. 'Aren't you taking a lot for granted?' she retorted in an attempt at self-preservation. 'Yes, of course I like you or I wouldn't be here. But, as I told your foster-mother we're just friends.'

'Fine! And that's how it has to stay, because our ways of life are totally incompatible.'

There was so much tumult inside her she felt physically sick. 'What a stupid thing to say! Our ways of life are exactly the same. I work at the hospital and so do you. How can that be incompatible?'

Grant sighed. 'I actually went to the lengths of looking up your father in *Who's Who*, Anne,' he explained. 'A fair old entry—prestigious family background, distinguished Army career, now a merchant banker—he might well end up being Lord Mayor one day. You and I are worlds apart. I wouldn't find it at all difficult to get fond of you, but I don't intend to fall into that trap. I'm not going to have it said that I'm chasing money and influence.'

She'd had an inkling that this might be the trouble. 'Well, aren't you the prize twit?' she declared. 'What the hell does it matter who my father is or what your background is?'

'Oh, it matters, Anne, as you'd very well know if you'd ever been on my side of the fence. I've got no wealthy father or rich relatives to feather my bed. My only fortune is in my hands.'

'Well, it certainly isn't in your brains tonight! You've made your own way in the world, and I should have thought that was something to be proud of. But never mind,' she tossed her head angrily and jumped up, 'who said I wanted to be more than friends anyway?'

Grant rose also, smiled ruefully and shook his head. 'I don't think I played that too well, did I? Sorry.'

'Forgiven,' she said, over-brightly. 'You may be a clever chap, Grant Ryder, but you're thick as two planks when it comes to women.' Reaching up, she kissed him lightly on the lips.

He sighed. 'You see what I mean—one kiss can lead to another, if you let it.'

'Oh, don't be so stuffy and don't read anything into *that* kiss. We South Ken kids kiss all our friends. OK?'

'Right. So long as we know where we're at.' He took her hand then, and they walked back down to the country pub.

Over a plate of moussaka and a glass of wine they talked about other things, leaving aside the vexed question of personal relationships. But it was brittle conversation with both of them treading carefully. And for all they had pushed it under the mat, for Anne the alchemy was there stronger than ever. Just to be near him sent her into a spate of longing. *He* might be tough enough to deny his feelings, but how was *she* going to cope with his rejection?

It was the most ghastly journey home she'd ever known, in spite of cheerful music on the car radio. She wanted to crawl away by herself and howl. How could she fight his indomitable pride? He couldn't really have deep feelings for her or he'd never let such a ridiculous thing as money or lack of it come between them.

When they came to her flat it was barely ten o'clock.

'Well, that was an interesting day,' she said, forcing a smile. 'Do you want coffee? I promise I want seduce you.'

Grant chuckled. 'No, I'll be getting along—a busy schedule tomorrow. Are you in?'

'Yes, but not on the ward. We've a study day. Georges is giving us a lecture on mechanical ventilation and trachy care.'

'Oh, right. See you around some time. And thanks for . . . well, for being you. I feel happier now we understand each other.'

'Yes, it was as well to clear the air,' she agreed, 'but will you do something for me . . . please.'

'What now?' he asked.

'Give me an enormous hug, like your foster-mother gave you. I've never been hugged like that in my whole life.'

He laughed. 'Oh, Anne, you make it sound as though *you* had a deprived childhood! Come here!' And he took her in his arms and gave her a terrific bear-hug with an accompanying growl. 'That do?'

'For the time being,' she said. 'I may want a top-up now and again. That much you owe me, having shown me what I missed. 'Bye.'

They had parted on a laugh, but once she was indoors Anne's defences crumbled and she let the tears flow. She felt lonely and abandoned. Grant had given her an affectionate hug, but there were definitely no sexual overtones and no kisses. She didn't know what she'd been hoping for, but his self-control was total.

Perhaps it was a good thing he had been blunt. At least she knew where she stood. They had established some kind of footing and being confessed friends was surely better than nothing at all. Oh, for someone to confide in! But Mandy was miles away, and Michelle was always too full of her own affairs to lend a sympathetic ear.

Maybe he would wake up one day and realise what a fool he had been.

'Fat chance!' she told herself dispiritedly. There was always that other woman—whoever she was—he had said was out of reach. Of course, he *could* have been joshing about that, in an effort to put her off.

She abandoned her attempt at trying to read his mind. Perhaps throwing herself into work was the only solution. Losing herself in other people's problems might help to blot out her pain. Probably that was what the admirable Ruth had done after finding she couldn't have children. There was a place for everybody somewhere in the world.

At the moment, though, her philosophising was cold comfort.

CHAPTER EIGHT

GETTING together with the other Neuro course nurses for their study day was good therapy for Anne, since it required her undivided attention. Their lecturer was Georges Alain who, as anaesthetist, was always involved with patients needing assisted breathing techniques. His fractured English and French charm brought a lighter note to this rather heavy subject.

Thoughts of Grant were pushed to the back of Anne's mind, until Hazel mentioned his name when the nurses finished the day with their usual get-together at the Jolly Friars.

'Hey, I saw you going off with Grant Ryder the other night, Anne. Anything to report?' she queried archly.

Anne laughed. 'For goodness' sake, one can't even have a drink with someone in this place without eyebrows rocketing! We're just good friends!' she clowned, to the amusement of the others.

Normally Anne would have enjoyed their confab, but tonight she was glad when Mrs Shore, their tutor, and Georges came to join them, which put paid to anything more than cheerful repartee.

Back at her flat and writing up her notes later that evening, Anne was interrupted by a phone call from her sister.

Michelle went on endlessly about her day out with Brad. 'We had a wonderful time, Annie. He was really impressed with Blenheim Palace. Well, it is impressive, isn't it? His camera never stopped clicking. We had dinner at that riverside place at Bray on the way home. It was *so* romantic!' Her laugh tinkled out. 'He paid me the most outrageous compliments, and I'm committed to show him Windsor next, when we're both free. By the way, I did invite him to Daddy's ball and he's keen to come. Did you get around to asking Grant?'

'Yes, and it's fine with him too. How shall we go . . . separately or together?' Anne asked.

'O-oh separately, I should think. Brad's got his own wheels now.' Michelle suddenly went off at a tangent. 'Oh! I thought you might like to know everything's fixed with your Professor Drapper, and our programme's all set to go out next month. As you said, I think he's going to be a find.'

'Great! Give the girl an Oscar!' Anne joked.

'Yes! Joe is really pleased—well, as much as Joe admits to being satisfied with *any*thing *anyone* does. Brad says I mustn't let him get to me. He says Joe's basically insecure, which is why he tries to come over as butch. Makes sense, doesn't it? That's why he stays with that little creep Hilary—she's his ego-stroker.'

Anne listened with a patient smile as her sister rattled on. There was scarcely the need to say anything herself, apart from the odd 'yes' and 'no'.

When she had finally finished talking about her own affairs Michelle thought to ask what, if anything, was happening in her sister's world.

'Not a lot,' Anne said lightly.

'Oh! No development between you and the blue-eyed boy, then?'

'If you mean Grant, no . . . at least, not the kind of development you're thinking of. He did take me to a birthday party yesterday, though.'

'Oh, well, play it cool. Come the ball and soft lights and sweet music, who knows what may happen?' Michelle returned. 'Look, Annie, will you ring Daddy and let him know who we're bringing? I'm frantically busy at the moment and he's so elusive. I can't spare the time to go chasing him.'

Anne promised that she would try and did so there and then, while she remembered. Their father was not at his home in Chatswood Gardens, but she tracked him down at his club.

'Splendid,' Sir Randolph said. 'Let me make a note of those names, if you'll spell them out to me. And who are these young men?' he enquired as he wrote. 'What are their backgrounds? Anything I need to know?'

'Grant is a senior neurosurgeon at St Martin's,' she told him, 'and Bradley Stevens is a doctor visiting from America. You'll like them, Daddy. They're nice guys.'

'Hmm! I've no doubt your Aunt Laura will cast her critical eye over them,' her father replied. 'Jonathan and his wife will also be with us, which will complete our table. It should be an agreeable party. I'll put your invitations in the post.'

When they had finished speaking Anne went back to her lecture notes, but found it hopeless trying to keep her mind on her work. Finally she abandoned the effort and set about tackling her accumulation of washing-up instead, during which she could let her thoughts wander at will.

In a way she was pleased that Jonathan and his wife were to be among her father's guests. With his wife present Jon's behaviour would be moderated to some extent, but it would do Grant no harm to see that her ex-boss still had a soft spot for her. And, as Michelle had pointed out, Grant might find himself not totally immune to the seductive influence of soft lights and sweet music. After rinsing out a pile of tights she went to bed in a more optimistic frame of mind.

'Cor, I dunno what's wrong with that Mr Wells this morning,' the ward maid grumbled. Millie had paused at the door of the sluice where Anne was testing early morning urine samples. 'I took him his fresh water jug and he asked me to fetch a bottle. When I said as it wasn't my job and what did his last servant die of—only joking like—he fair bit my head off. "Shut your face!" he says. Cheek!'

'Oh?' Anne frowned. 'That's not a bit like Mr Wells, Millie, he's usually such a dear old boy.'

'Yeah, I know. That's what I thought, until just now. You can 'ave my share of him today, though.'

'All right, Millie, I'll go and see him. Perhaps he's not feeling too good.'

Leaving her testing for the time being, Anne took

a urinal from the rack and went to check on her elderly patient, who normally would have used the bathroom. Routine ten a.m. observations had not yet been started, but casting her mind back to the night report she recalled no mention of any problems with Mr Wells. Indeed, he was possibly for discharge in a day or two.

Coming to his bedside, she found him lying back against his pillows with his eyes closed. His craggy, bruised face was sweaty, his breathing seemed erratic and there was a blueness around his lips which was disturbing.

'Mr Wells,' Anne said gently, laying a hand on his arm, 'Millie said you asked for a bottle.'

He opened his rheumy blue eyes and gazed at her vacantly. Then he muttered, 'Silly cow . . . never did.' His lids drooped again, but not before she detected a slight enlargement of his right pupil.

As she laid her fingers on his pulse and timed it, her concern increased. 'Is your headache no better, Harold?' she asked.

'No, it ain't. Stop fussing, fer Gawd's sake,' he growled irritably when she raised his lids and shone her pencil torch into his eyes.

Anne left him and went to report her anxiety to Sister Glynn, but Mary was not in her office or anywhere else to be found.

Poking her head between the curtains around the bed of a hemiplegic patient who was being bed-bathed by Hazel with the help of a student nurse, she said, 'Excuse me, but do you know where Sister Mary is?'

'Yes, gone to see the gynae consultant about something. If you want the keys they're in my pocket,' Hazel indicated, smoothing her side of the sheet.

'Damn!' Anne muttered. 'I'm worried about Mr Wells . . . he's showing signs of cerebral compression. I think we ought to get Bob here. Come and have a look, would you?'

'OK . . . be back in a minute, Joan,' Hazel told her assistant, and she went with Anne to give her opinion.

'Mr Wells, can you open your eyes for me?' she asked. He muttered something unintelligible and his lids fluttered open briefly, then closed again. When she asked him if he could squeeze her hand he did so after a fashion. The corners of Hazel's mouth turned down. 'Slow to respond, Annie. Yeah, I'd call Bob if I were you. Mary may not like it, but she'd like it even less if things got worse and she got a rocket for not reporting it sooner. Better be safe than sorry.'

'Yes, that's what I thought,' said Anne.

The houseman was with Grant in his outpatients' clinic when he answered her bleep, and before she knew it she found herself speaking to the registrar herself, relaying her findings of increasing intracranial pressure.

'Right,' he said, 'keep him under obs and we'll be along.'

The doctors arrived within ten minutes, by which time Mr Wells's condition had deteriorated even further. Events moved quickly then.

'A subdural haematoma, Bob?' Grant conjectured after making his examination. 'We'll have to go in and investigate. We've got a consent form signed, have we?' He glanced at Anne. 'And his blood cross-matched?'

'Yes, Group O, Rh-positive,' she said, turning up the information in the notes.

'Right,' Grant reacted with his usual brisk authority. 'We'll fix up a theatre. No time for much prepping, Anne, but shave this area of his head, will you?' His large, gentle hand smoothed the patient's scant grey hair. 'Not that there's much to come off,' he murmured kindly. 'I'll give you a buzz when we're ready for him.'

The doctors went away to make their preparations and Hazel joined Anne to help with what she had to do. His false teeth had already been removed as his symptoms worsened. He was not rousable now, but the nurses talked him through their actions all the same. Finally, after having done as much as they could, they put him into an operating gown and checked that his identification labels were intact.

A message came that the porters were on their way to collect him and by eleven o'clock Anne accompanied her patient to theatre for emergency investigation of a possible blood clot. Although it seemed pointless, she held his hand en route and talked to him encouragingly, explaining where he was going and that soon he'd be feeling better. That, at least, was what she hoped for as she left him with the staff in the anaesthetics-room and went back to the ward in sombre mood.

Mary also had by now arrived back and was not at all disturbed by what had gone on in her absence. In fact she was in remarkable good humour. 'Well, at least you appear to have learned something since you've been here,' she said. 'You have to keep your eyes open and act quickly on this ward.'

With unaccustomed frankness she went on to talk about her own interview with the gynaecological consultant. 'I've got a uterine fibroid, he says. Nothing more serious than that, thank God!' She put her hands together and rolled her eyes heavenwards.

'Oh, I am sorry. I didn't know you'd been having trouble,' Anne sympathised. 'Is he going to whip it out for you?'

'Yes, as soon as he can. I shall have to arrange for my husband to take some time off to look after our boy.' Mary went back to being her old officious self and began sorting importantly through some test results on her desk. 'Make sure Mr Wells's bed is ready, then you can go to first lunch.'

Anne paused on her way out. 'We haven't yet told his daughter about this emergency. Will you do that? She is on the telephone.'

Mary waved her hand impatiently. 'Right, find me the number and I'll get on to her.'

Having written out the number and put it in front of the sister, Anne prepared the operation bed in the customary manner and then went off to lunch in the company of Hazel.

'I do hope there'll be no brain damage for that

poor old chap,' she confided. 'I shall feel worse than awful if I've landed his daughter with a chronic invalid.'

'Don't be daft,' Hazel returned, 'no one could have reacted quicker than you did. With any luck he'll be all right.'

Anne smiled wanly. 'Anyway, now I shall appreciate more how doctors feel when their efforts prove less than satisfactory.'

'Well, the books say that once a clot is evacuated the recovery can be quite dramatic, and Mary seemed pleased that we'd coped without her, didn't she?' Hazel pointed out.

Over their snack lunch the nurses discussed the sister and her fibroid.

'Maybe that's why she's as offhand as she sometimes is. Maybe she'd been worrying. You never know what pressures people are labouring under,' Anne pondered.

To everyone's delight, by two-thirty that afternoon Mr Wells was back in the ward, his head encased in bandages, but his clot successfully drained. His pupils were now equal and reacting, and although he was still drowsy after an injection for pain relief, he was responding normally to questions and stimuli.

It was with a sense of wonder that Anne realised she had actually helped to avert a disaster, and she sailed through the rest of the day in a state of euphoria. She felt even more elated when, reporting off duty at four-thirty, she found Grant in the office with Mary, and he couldn't have been nicer.

'My goodness, you're looking pleased with life!' he remarked, glancing up from the case notes he was writing and flashing her a wry smile.

'Well, so I should be,' she returned blithely. 'It's not every day one's favourite patient is snatched from the jaws of death.'

'No. A good feeling isn't it?'

They exchanged grins and Anne left for her two days off, so heartened by his manner that she could have burst into song. She knew she had pleased him, although he hadn't said as much. Her part had been minor compared with his skill, but it was a vital part all the same. She had helped him to beat the last enemy.

The following day, still in cheerful mood, Anne took herself on a shopping spree to the West End and bought a new dress for the ball. She chose a summery gown in soft orchid-pink silk with an off-the-shoulder bodice and a swirling skirt. She had just returned home and unpacked her purchase when her flatmate arrived back from Devon.

'Mandy! Great to see you!' Anne exclaimed as her friend struggled into their living-room with bulging travel-bag. 'Oh, I've really missed you. Why didn't you let me know you were coming? I'd have killed the fatted calf. How's the foot?'

Mandy flopped down on the sofa, kicked off her trainers and peeled off a sock to show Anne her scar. 'Made a good job of it, didn't they? It's still a bit tender, but not too bad if I wear a sponge sock in my shoe. Hey, you've been spending some money!' she said, nodding towards the dress which was lying among the tissue paper in its box. 'That looks gorgeous . . . what's it in aid of?'

'Long story,' Anne laughed. 'I'll tell you presently. Do you want to go out for a meal, or shall we make do with what's in the fridge?'

'Oh, I don't feel like going out again. Let's make do. Besides, Colin promised to ring me this evening.'

'Colin being the knight in the bloody white trousers, I suppose?' Anne teased. 'It's still on then, the love story of the year?'

'You bet!' Mandy ran her hands through her spiky brown hair. 'Oh, Annie, he's terrific,' she sighed. 'Honestly, I know I've not known him long, but it just hit me between the eyes. Somehow you just know when a thing's right, don't you?'

'Yes. It must be terrific when you both feel the same way,' Anne said pensively.

Mandy eyed her friend askance. 'It takes one lovesick dope to recognise another,' she observed. 'Who is it . . . the neurosurgical reg?'

'Oh, God! How did you guess? Have people been talking?'

'Nobody's been talking. You mentioned him yourself in glowing terms that time you were telling me about your sister and the American guy. I can add up! You were impressed with him from the beginning, weren't you?'

Anne sighed heavily. 'Yes, I suppose so, but I

never realised I should get to feeling like this about him. Mandy, he won't have me,' she despaired, 'and it's all because our family backgrounds are different. Oh, it's so ridiculous, it's unbelievable. I could *scream!*'

Mandy scratched her head, looking puzzled. 'Sounds a strange sort of reason. I should have thought your background would have measured up to anybody's.'

'It's the other way about, pal,' Anne said with a short laugh. 'A case of I've been feather-bedded all my life and he's got where he is by his own sweat.'

'Oh-oh! Pride with a capital P. Tricky, but people have crossed bigger divides than that. Let's have a coffee and you can tell me about it.'

Anne made the drinks and unburdened herself about the way things were. It was a relief just to be able to talk to someone after having had to bottle up her feelings.

'I *know* he likes me, Mandy. He as good as admitted it, but he laid it on the line that he was only interested in friendship. So, naturally, I said that's all *I* was interested in anyway. He didn't really believe me, I could tell. And I can't see him without wanting him. And it's hell,' Anne finished miserably.

'Yeah, I know what you mean,' Mandy sympathised. 'It's the same with me and Colin, only fortunately he wants me too. I don't know what to suggest,' she said, 'except wait and see. If he feels as strongly as you do perhaps *he* won't be able to settle for friendship.'

'Do me a favour,' scoffed Anne. 'He's got so much wretched will-power that if I danced naked in front of him he'd probably shut his eyes and order me to put some clothes on.'

Mandy chuckled. 'I wouldn't bet on that! So what's this glamorous creation for?' she asked, lifting out the dress and holding it against herself.

Anne explained, and her flatmate pursed her lips. 'Well, that can't be bad. He'll probably be your adoring slave before the night's out.'

'If only!' Anne sighed. But it was an encouraging thought.

The gilt-edged invitations to the ball arrived early the next week. Anne slipped Grant's into her shoulder-bag, hoping to be able to give it to him some time beforehand, to remind him of time and place. She brushed with him fleetingly on the ward from time to time, but the right moment never came. Indeed, apart from one occasion, she might have thought he was being deliberately cool with her.

It was a week since Mr Wells's emergency surgery. Anne had removed his stitches earlier that day and he was back to being more like his former agreeable self. During visiting hours she was having a word at the bedside with the old man and his daughter when Grant came to the ward to check on another patient.

He paused at the foot of the bed and smiled at the young woman and her father. 'Well, sir,' he said, 'I hear our social worker is busy trying to find you some sheltered accommodation, just as soon as you're well enough to leave us.'

'Yes, doc,' Mr Wells nodded, 'she said she had something in mind. P'raps falling down the stairs did me a bit of good after all.'

The neurosurgeon laughed. 'Not really to be recommended, at any age. If it hadn't been for the sharp eyes of our nursing staff you might not be needing any kind of accommodation!'

'Oh, I know you all had to get your skates on,' the old man said. 'Thanks very much for what you did.'

'That's what we're here for.' Grant flung a teasing smile in Anne's direction. 'I expect Nurse Westlake had her fingers crossed for you. She does that for the lads she takes a fancy to.'

'I planted a feather as well, don't forget!' Anne returned, joining in the joke.

Their eyes met. There was a sudden commotion in her breast when she recalled that warm Sunday evening in Epping Forest and the things that were said between them. She wondered if he remembered it too.

His gaze returned to his patient. 'Don't worry, Mr Wells, we don't pin our faith entirely on lucky charms . . . and she doesn't ride a broomstick!' Grinning, he strolled away, loose-limbed and virile.

Mr Wells's daughter gazed after the tall, macho doctor, approval lighting her eyes. She had been quiet in his presence, now she spoke up. 'I like 'im,' she said. 'Ever so nice to me, he was. Not like some

. . . too big to talk to you.'

Anne agreed. 'No, he always makes himself available. He'll talk to anyone.' Anyone except me, at the moment, she brooded mournfully.

The days slipped by until Thursday and Anne had still not managed to have a private moment with Grant. It even crossed her mind that he might have forgotten their date. That was until she met Brad in one of the corridors on her way to tea.

Greeting her warmly, he stopped to talk. 'Hi, honey! How's life?'

'Fine,' she smiled. 'I hear you and Michelle had a good day out last Sunday. Thanks for that, Brad. She doesn't get a lot of opportunity to unwind.'

'My pleasure entirely,' Brad enthused. 'I could get real fond of your sister,' he went on with a sportive shake of his head. 'She's a handful, but she's a swell lady. Hey, what about this ball on Saturday? That should be a real nice occasion, as I was saying to Grant in the mess last night.'

'Oh, he has remembered, then?' said Anne.

'Sure he's remembered. I showed him the invitation which Michelle sent to me, and he mentioned he hadn't received his yet.'

'No, I've got it here.' Anne fished in her shoulder-bag. 'It seemed ridiculous to post it when I see him almost daily. I've just not had a moment to give it to him. If you're seeing him, would you mind . . .?'

'OK, Anne, will do.' Brad stuffed the envelope in the pocket of his white coat, and after a few more pleasantries they parted.

Problem solved! she thought happily. Now it would be up to Grant to contact *her* to make arrangements.

She worked until nine-thirty that night and when she got back to the flat Mandy said, with an arch look, 'Guess who's been ringing you-hoo?'

Anne's heart began to drum, but she said, levelly, 'Grant, I suppose?'

'Grant, she supposes!' returned Mandy, laughing. 'Gosh, if that was Colin ringing me, I'd be doing cartwheels! I thought you were supposed to be nuts on the guy?'

'I'm trying not to be,' Anne sighed. 'And don't get excited . . . I expect he only rang about the invitation for Saturday which I gave Brad to give to him.'

'Well, he wants you to ring him back. Number's on the pad.'

Anne got into her dressing-gown and made herself a drink before she dialled Grant's number.

'Ryder here,' the vibrant tones came over the wire.

'Hi, Grant. It's me, Anne,' she said.

'Oh, Anne,' he returned, 'I wanted to know whether our date for Saturday is still on?'

'Yes, of course it is.' She was a little mystified. 'Brad gave you the invitation, didn't he?'

After a slight pause, he replied, 'No . . . he showed me his last night, but as far as I'm aware there wasn't one for me.'

'Well, he didn't have it then,' she explained. 'I gave it to him this afternoon and he promised to pass it on.'

'I see!' Grant's tone of voice implied the exact opposite. 'Why did we need a go-between? I do have an office, and a secretary, and I'm not made of ectoplasm. Why couldn't you have given it to me yourself?'

'For goodness' sake,' she laughed, 'does it matter, so long as you get it? I happened to see Brad, and it seemed simpler to give it to him than run around the hospital looking for you.'

He growled a bit, then said, 'All right, I expect he'll give it to me when I see him tomorrow. What time would you like me to pick you up?'

'Six-thirtyish?' she suggested. 'It's seven for seven-thirty, but it won't take us long to get there. Er—would you rather we had a taxi from here, to save you having to stay on the wagon?'

'No, I shan't go over the top,' he assured her. 'I drink very little these days. Too much at stake for me to take risks.'

'OK, it's up to you,' she said.

'Listen, in case you were looking for me tomorrow, I shan't be at the hospital. Brad and I are going to a symposium in Oxford, but we'll be back by Saturday. And another thing, Anne, next time you've something for me, deliver it in person, will you? There's no need to avoid me because of that conversation we had last week.'

'Well, that's rich!' she protested. 'It hasn't been *me* doing the avoiding. You've hardly spared the time to give me a nod of your head since last week. I thought that was the way you wanted it.'

'All right, I'll overlook it this time,' he said.

'Gee, thanks. I'm underwhelmed! Well, enjoy your symposium. 'Bye-ee!'

'And just what was all that about?' Mandy asked in bewilderment.

Anne sighed heavily, shrugging her shoulders. '*He's* allowed to cool it if and when it suits him, but he objects when I do. Men!'

Her flatmate laughed. 'They're all misunderstood little boys at heart, Annie.'

CHAPTER NINE

WITH Mandy now back at work and on a late, Anne again had their flat to herself that Saturday evening as she prepared for her glamorous night out with Grant. Fresh and fragrant after her bath, she slid into her new orchid-pink silk dress. The sensuous touch of the gossamer fabric flowing over her limbs heightened her expectations of the pleasures ahead.

Studying herself in front of the full-length mirror, she was well pleased with her choice. The colour complemented the soft radiance of her skin and her starry eyes told her she looked attractive. Humming along to the tune on the radio, she brushed her glossy blonde hair into its well-cut casual style before fastening on a pair of glittering pendant earrings. 'I just called to say I love you,' the singer crooned. Any time now Grant would be calling to pick her up. Perhaps, one day, he might get around to saying such things to her, if only he could get that chip off his shoulder, about differing family backgrounds. Well, tonight promised to be a magical night—one when anything might happen. The bubble of excitement inside her grew.

Moments late she opened the door to his ring. Debonair and handsome in black evening dress, Grant looked her over appreciatively and gave a soft wolf-whistle.

Her breath came quickly. Oh, if only she could have thrown her arms around him as she longed to do, instead of having to go through this farce of platonic friendship!

'Hi!' she said, with a bright smile, letting him into the small hall. 'So you made it back from Oxford all right?'

He lifted one dark brow, his blue eyes twinkling. 'Would I have dared not to?'

Anne laughed. 'Oh, nothing surprises me any more. I'm growing used to fickle fate.' His appraising gaze was making her self-conscious. 'Shall we go?' she said, and draping her matching shawl about her bare shoulders, she followed him out to his car.

'Your carriage, my lady!' Grant opened the door of his Escort with a flourish.

She stood back for a moment in mock admiration at the gleaming maroon paintwork. 'My goodness, what a polish!'

'Yes, I gave her a birthday in your honour. Although you should be riding in a Rolls in that rig-out.'

Seated beside his powerful body as they drove towards London's West End, Anne couldn't remember when she had last felt so elated. It was a long time since she'd been to a really special occasion in the company of such a thrilling partner.

'I had my twenty-first at the Café Royal,' she said, breaking the silence between them, 'only in a smaller suite than the one we shall be in tonight. A lot has changed since that day,' she sighed.

Grant replied with a half-smile, 'It's almost too long ago for me to remember mine. A rather boisterous, boozy affair with some of my mates . . . and the following week we started on the wards.'

In contrast to the damp and overcast evening the atmosphere inside the car was pleasant enough and she found they were talking easily.

'Weren't you scared about getting to grips with real patients instead of just textbook stuff? I know I was,' she said.

He shook his dark classic head. 'Good heavens, no! I couldn't wait to begin. People have always fascinated me. That's one of the reasons why I'm looking forward to tonight. Observing strangers is an interesting occupation.'

She should have known better than to ask, Anne thought, when everything about him spelled confidence. She said jauntily, 'I hope you don't intend to spend the entire night putting people under the microscope. You are going to dance with me, aren't you? That's the only reason I asked you.'

Grant gave a crooked smile. 'Not entirely true, Miss Westlake. I wouldn't mind betting you got pushed into it by your sister. I should think she's quite good at manipulating people.'

Her pink mouth rounded into an indignant, 'Oh, that's unfair! You hardly know her. You shouldn't make snap judgements.'

'It doesn't take much intelligence to see that you're the giver and she's the taker,' he observed drily.

'Michelle has her good points,' Anne defended,

her chin in the air. 'She's had a rough deal, don't forget.'

'OK, Michelle's had a rough deal, and I admire you for your loyalty. Shall we leave it at that?'

She was thoughtful for a moment, trying to put herself in his place. Not having family ties, how could he be expected to understand that strange, indefinable blood bond which welded you together through the bad times as well as the good and made allowances for failings?

'Do you remember much about your parents?' she asked with a sideways glance at his strong profile.

'Bits. I remember most about my father, because we had three years together. I might have had a brother or sister if my mother hadn't been killed. She was pregnant at the time, he told me.' Grant changed the subject by asking roguishly, 'If I hadn't come tonight who would you have invited? Surely not that fellow you used to work for?'

'*Jonathan?*' She laughed. 'No, although he's good company and he'll be in our party tonight . . . he and his wife.'

'Oh, married, is he?'

'Yes, to Belinda, who keeps producing sons when he's longing for a daughter.'

Grant chuckled. 'Too bad! Not her fault, though. It's his part in the business which decides the sex.'

'Fortunately for him, she's the original earth mother,' Anne said. 'So long as he's prepared to go on trying, she's prepared to go on having babies, or so I'm led to believe.'

'Lucky for some!' Grant concentrated on easing the car through the traffic streaming around Piccadilly Circus, and finally drew to a halt outside the entrance to the famous restaurant. 'If you'd like to go ahead,' he said, 'I'll find somewhere to park.'

'OK, fine. See you later.'

A commissionaire stepped forward to hold the door for her and she gave him a warm smile of thanks as she went in.

Other cars arriving deposited other guests resplendent in rustling silks, satins, furs and sparkling jewellery. There was an impressive mix of entertainment personalities and well-known socialites.

'*Anne!* Long time no see!' trilled an aristocratic voice when she entered the superbly-appointed ladies' powder room.

'Hello, Imogen,' Anne smiled at the tall, angular girl whom she used to meet at parties before her nursing career began. 'Yes, it's ages, isn't it?'

'Where are you hiding yourself these days?' the other girl asked.

'Well, I'm not hiding exactly, but my job keeps me busy.'

'Oh, yes, I did hear that you were being frightfully noble . . . nursing the sick and all that.'

Anne laughed. 'No, not noble at all. It's just a lot more interesting than what I was doing before.' She was rather glad that Michelle sailed in at that moment and, as usual, monopolised the conversation.

The zip, she said, had got stuck on the new dress she had bought for the occasion '. . . so I've had to make do with this,' she mourned, adjusting the top of her sensational strapless blue-green shot silk model.

'Well, I haven't seen that one before, and it looks gorgeous,' Anne assured her.

Michelle fluffed out her rich, dark hair and preened herself in the mirror. 'Brad said he actually liked it better. But then he would, wouldn't he?'

Anne chuckled. 'Good psychology, you mean?'

'Yes. I wasn't born yesterday. I can read him as well as he reads me.' Michelle grinned. 'All the same, he's a pet. Come on. Daddy and Aunt Laura are here. I saw them as I came in.'

Both their partners were waiting outside the reception lounge when the girls went through. After friendly greetings to their opposite escorts, they posed for pictures by the official photographer and were then announced, and received by their distinguished hosts for the evening.

Looking about her, Anne saw the dignified, silver-haired figure of their father over by the table plan. With him was their Aunt Laura, stately in a cloth-of-gold gown, and they were talking to Jonathan and his full-bosomed wife.

Introductions made, Sir Randolph enquired courteously whether the American was enjoying his stay in England.

'Very much, sir, and your daughters are making it all the more enjoyable,' Brad declared gallantly.

'Flattery will get you nowhere,' retorted Michelle, 'especially when I don't have a drink.' She spread her graceful hands pathetically.

'Oh, sorry, honey. What would you like . . . what would everyone like?' Brad enquired. Having committed their requests to memory, he went off, with Jon to help, towards the cocktail bar.

Grant, meanwhile, had been engaged in conversation by Aunt Laura. Anne gave him an impish sideways glance. She would have loved to eavesdrop, but Belinda claimed her attention.

'What a gorgeous guy!' Jon's wife murmured, watching the surgeon, her pebble-grey eyes curious. 'Where did you find him?'

'I work with him at St Martin's. He's the one who operated on Mr Carle after his collapse at Ascot—I expect Jon will have told you about that. You were having your baby at the time. How is your new little boy?' Anne asked.

Belinda was only too happy to talk about her latest child and went on to say how pleased she was with the new nanny, and what a problem it was deciding on names, and on godparents, and the difficulties involved in getting one's figure back. 'But I'm forgetting diets for tonight,' she declared as their drinks arrived.

Dinner was announced and the company filed into the splendid banqueting hall with its gilded mirrored walls, glittering chandeliers and round, flower-decked tables. Anne's place setting was between her father and Jonathan—two seats removed from Grant. She caught his eye, and he smiled at her in between paying polite attention to her aunt on his right and Belinda on his left. He appeared quite at ease and thoroughly enjoying himself.

Anne, for her part, could hardly wait for the meal and the speeches to be over so that she could have her share of his company. Her father was his usual quiet self, but Jonathan was as flirtatious as ever.

'Now, take your beautiful green eyes off the good doctor and pay a little attention to me!' he teased, tweaking a strand of her hair.

'Oh, sorry,' she laughed, starting on her *Sole bonne femme*, 'I was miles away.'

'Yes, I know you were. I was saying how delightful you look. I might be inspired to write poetry if you still worked for me.'

She laughed. 'Jonathan, you're an idiot! You get worse as you get older.' But she was quite pleased that Grant happened to be looking in her direction while Jon was being attentive.

At long last the coffee and liqueurs stage arrived, the invited celebrity said his piece in praise of the donations to charitable trusts, and the ladies retired to repair their make-up before dancing began.

'My dear, what a nice young man your friend is,' Aunt Laura remarked to her niece. 'He was so interested in my work for prisoners' families. I asked him if he was connected with the Ryders of Poultney Park, and he said no, Manor Park. Is that the latest "in" place to live these days?'

Anne smiled to herself, imagining how Grant would have been amused by the question. 'I wouldn't know,' she said, 'I only see him at the hospital. But I do know he lost both his parents when he was quite young.'

'Really? Well, it doesn't appear to have done him any harm.' Aunt Laura resited a diamanté-studded comb in her well-dressed brown hair. 'Has he any prospects?'

'As a neurosurgeon, plenty, I should think,' said Anne, but she was well aware that wasn't quite what her aunt had in mind.

Back in the ballroom, when Anne and her companions returned, the prestigious dance band was striking up with their first number. Grant, who had been talking at the table with the other men, rose on seeing Anne. 'One dancing partner, ready, willing and able,' he joshed. 'Shall we?' and he whirled her into the quickstep.

At first they simply danced. There was no need to talk as he swung her skilfully around the floor. Their bodies moved in blissful harmony. Then she said, smiling up at him, 'I noticed you were getting on very well with my Aunt Laura.'

'That's my job, isn't it, to get on with people,' Grant replied lightly. 'Dukes or dustmen . . . makes no difference to me. Seriously, she's a nice lady, filling her life with good works. I imagine the benefit is two-way.'

'Yes . . . it makes her feel useful,' Anne agreed. 'She was going to be married a long time ago, but her fiancé was killed on manoeuvres. He was in the Army.'

'That must have happened to a lot of women of her generation,' he reflected.

As they continued dancing, his powerful body

so near to hers filled Anne with ardent longing. She was amazed by the intensity of her own desire. She found she wanted him with a passion she hardly believed herself capable of. Presently she said, in a small voice, 'Isn't that an argument for taking what's on offer . . . in case tomorrow never comes?' Apart from actually saying *I love you*, she couldn't have put her feelings more plainly, and her cheeks flamed.

Grant held her a little away, looking down at her with a quizzical expression on his strong, intelligent face. He said gently, 'That's only one side of the coin, Anne. Suppose tomorrow came . . . and in the cold light of day you wished you'd thought twice?' He kissed the hand he was holding, then smiled. 'I think this debate would be better another day, when the effect of your champagne has worn off.'

Anne felt both crushed and humiliated. 'A glass or two of Bollinger is hardly likely to rob me of my wits, but have it your way.' She bit her lips as her throat tightened. Right, that's it, Grant Ryder! she thought stormily. I as good as offered myself to you, but if that's your ridiculous attitude, you've had it!

After that she avoided him. She sought out her father for the next dance, then she danced with Brad, and several times with Jonathan, who was a satisfying partner in every way—except that he wasn't the man she wanted.

Time was getting on when the orchestra played the tune she had heard while she was dressing earlier that evening—'I just called to say I love you'. Grant came to her before anyone else could forestall him, clasping his hands behind her waist, so that she had no option but to put hers on his shoulders. 'It's been a terrific evening, hasn't it?' he murmured.

'I'm glad you've enjoyed it,' she said frigidly.

'Haven't you?'

'So-so.'

'Why . . . what's wrong? Everyone's been dancing attendance on you . . . especially the Honourable Jonathan Locke,' he added, an ironic twist to his shapely lips. 'What more could you want?'

'Nothing . . . nothing at all!' she returned, her cool smile at odds with her clamouring heart.

'Fine! Then why the frost?' When she didn't answer he pulled her a little closer and murmured, 'You can't always have everything you want, you know.' And the male vocalist, putting his heart into the words of the song, destroyed the last bastion of her self-control.

Biting her lips, she somehow managed to choke back the tears until the number ended, then she excused herself and made a dash for the cloakroom.

It was fortunately empty, save for the cloakroom attendant, who threw Anne a curious look as she sat at a dressing-table, grabbed a pink tissue from the box and blew her nose vigorously.

'Are you all right, madam?' the woman asked.

'Oh, yes, thank you,' Anne returned with a wan smile, 'just a bit of a headache.' She accepted the offer of a paracetamol and washed it down with a glass of cold water. 'Thank you . . . you're very kind.'

'My pleasure, madam,' the attendant said. 'I expect it's the noise in there—enough to split your ear-drums sometimes, isn't it?'

Having regained her composure, Anne went back to the ballroom where the tempo had begun to accelerate as the evening drew to its close. Streamers and popping balloons surrounded the revellers, and she was sucked into the general carousing before the last dance was announced.

Her father and Aunt Laura decided to slip away before it began, and after expressing their thanks for a happy time the younger element got on with the serious business of finishing the evening in proper style.

Michelle and Brad were as close as two people could possible get on the dance floor, Jonathan dutifully partnered his wife, and Grant drew Anne into his arms.

'Come on, this has probably got to last me a long time,' he said with a whimsical smile.

'That's entirely your own choice,' she returned.

'Anne,' he replied quietly, 'it's not my fault that our lives run on different tracks. Tonight has convinced me more than ever that it would be a mistake to let myself get deeply involved with you. Good grief! The hunting-shooting-fishing fraternity would drive me nuts in no time. I'll doctor them if they need me, but join them, never! I detest the breed.'

'What an unfair generalisation,' she scoffed. 'There are good and bad people in all walks of life.'

'Agreed. What I really meant was, let them go their way and I'll go mine.' He gave a short laugh. 'You're so sensible sometimes, I can hardly believe you're out of the same drawer.'

'Thanks very much, you pompous oaf. I'm not out of any particular drawer. I'm *me*. And the sooner you learn to stop pigeonholing people, the better!'

'Oh, dear! Why do I always put things so badly when I talk to you?' he sighed. 'What I should have said was, you're my kind of girl. And *if* it were possible . . . and *if* I were the marrying kind . . .'

'Oh, back to the embittered bachelor thing, are we?' she cut in with a careless laugh. 'Well, I think the girl who brought that on is well rid of you.'

'You never spoke a truer word, my dear, so count yourself lucky that I'm a man of principle.'

'I detest men of principle. They bore me.'

With that, he kissed her fiercely, robbing her of breath. 'Don't push me too far,' he warned, 'or you'll end up getting hurt.'

The party was over. There were fond farewells all round and an excess of kisses. With Brad having left his own car at Michelle's flat, they summoned a taxi to take them back there. Jonathan's chauffeur arrived and he and his wife were soon on their way. Anne waited in the entrance for Grant to bring his car around. Even at past one a.m. Piccadilly Circus was still full of light and life, but as they left the

West End the City streets became quieter save for the passing traffic.

Wrapped in her own unhappiness, Anne had little to say to the commanding figure beside her. It had obviously been a mistake inviting him tonight. It had made things worse between them, not better. Oh, how she longed for some wise counsellor to advise her what to do! Should she give up the Neuro course—go to some other hospital? Because she couldn't possibly work with this obstinate, proud man every day and stifle the rising tide of her love for him. It would go on smouldering. And how could she ever bear it if he married someone else?

'Wake up there,' Grant cut through her sombre thoughts as she chewed her thumbnail. 'I asked, is Brad going to stay the night at your sister's?'

'I don't know. We didn't discuss it.'

'Well, it might be the best thing. He wasn't exactly staying on the wagon, was he?'

Her only defence was in sarcasm. 'Whereas you are stone-cold sober, Mr Perfect.'

'Yes, I promised you I would be, and I am.'

'Spare me the heroics,' she said in a bored voice. 'What do you want, a medal?'

His stern jaw jutted ominously. 'I deserve a medal for keeping my temper with you! I feel sorely tempted to stop and slap your spoiled backside.'

'Good heavens! A reaction at last! Your trouble is,' she flared, 'you think you can make the rules and everyone else will fall into line. Well, count me out. *If* ever *I* marry, I certainly shan't be promising to *obey*.'

'In your present acid frame of mind no one will ever ask you,' he snapped back, bringing the car to a halt at traffic lights.

'Suits me. So that's two of us doomed to a lonely old age.'

They glared at each other. Then his grim mouth relaxed a little and he aimed a playful cuff at her chin. 'God help the man who ever gets hold of you!' he declared, rolling his eyes skywards.

The lights changed to green and he started forward again. Anne's eyes were fixed on the quiet road ahead. She had never felt so wretched. She didn't want to fight with him, yet she couldn't seem to help herself. A question of salvaging her own pride, she supposed. Absently she watched the unsteady gait of a ragged tramp shuffling along the pavement, a bottle in one hand. *And you think you've got problems!* she reproved herself.

It happened in a split second. One moment there the vagrant was, ambling uncertainly in their direction, and in the next instant he staggered into the road just a few yards ahead of them.

'Grant!' Anne screamed, her hands flying to her mouth.

There was no time to stop. He took the only course possible, wrenching the car sharply to the left and missing the tramp by inches. But Anne only felt the jolt as they bounced up the kerb and heard the crunch as the solid red pillar-box stopped their progress. After that she knew nothing.

CHAPTER TEN

IN HER green-curtained cubicle in a private corner of Women's Neurosurgical, Anne lay quietly studying the wavy pattern of the screens. It was not a good choice for a neuro ward, wavy lines, when your head was aching, she reflected absently. She closed her eyes to blot them out, but then the nightmare returned. She saw herself quarrelling with Grant . . . the drunk stepping into the path of the car . . . and the red pillar-box closing in on them before that final sickening crunch of metal on metal.

Sara's voice had been the first to break through to her dawning consciousness. She had recognised the Midlands voice saying, 'Annie, wake up, love. Squeeze my hand if you can hear me.'

Of course I can hear you, Anne had thought irritably, trying to pinpoint where she was. Then panic gripped her as a flash of memory took her back to those last few minutes before the crash. She, obviously, had survived, if her aching head and sore body were anything to go by. But what about Grant? Dear God . . . please don't let him be dead! was her silent, anguished prayer,

That was midday on Sunday, they had told her later. She'd been KO'd for about ten hours, but she was going to be fine. Professor Drapper had been there, putting her through the usual neurological tests.

'You've had a full scan, and there are no fractures anywhere,' he assured her. 'Apart from that nasty bump on your head, just a few bruised ribs and abrasions.' He beamed at her paternally. 'You'll be all right in a few days, my dear. A lucky escape you had, the pair of you.'

Gazing anxiously at other people around her bed, Anne had hardly dared to ask about her companion. 'Grant . . . h-how is he . . .?'

Georges Alain, who was also there, patted her hand understandingly. 'Don't worry, little one, e's OK. 'E was 'ere during the night, wiz your papa and your sister. We sent zem off to get some rest. They'll be back again soon.'

She saw their kindly faces through a mist as the welcome news sank in. Feelings of relief, remorse and gratitude overwhelmed her and she wept helplessly.

Sister Comfrey, a dedicated nurse with years of experience, made sympathetic noises and pulled some tissues from the box at the bedside. 'Here you are, dear. You'll be feeling better in a little while. Your flatmate has brought in your own nightie,' she went on, smoothing Anne's hair. 'We'll give you a nice wash in a minute, then you can settle down and have a proper rest.'

Since then the hours had passed in a kind of haze. Visitors came and went in between her periods of sleep—her father and Michelle, Brad, her nurse tutor—but it wasn't until after seven p.m. that she awoke to find Grant beside her bed with Sister

Comfrey.

His skilled fingers were on her pulse, and when she turned her wondering eyes towards him he simply said, 'Hello . . . how are you?' in that thrilling voice of his. Only his concerned gaze, meeting hers, betrayed the more intimate nature of his enquiry.

'I feel . . . like a human punch-bag,' she replied slowly, in a weak attempt at humour. 'How about you?'

'Oh, just a few bruises. I'm afraid you got the worst of it. However, it could have been much worse, couldn't it?' He paused before adding softly, 'Tomorrow *nearly* didn't come. You must have had *all* your fingers crossed last night!'

Anne found her eyes brimming with tears again and Sister Comfrey tutted and produced more tissues. 'There, there. It's all over now, and the only write-off was Mr Ryder's car.'

'Yes, even the tramp walked away unscathed,' said Grant.

She raised a tremulous smile. 'Glad about that, anyway.' There was so much more she wanted to say to him, but with the sister standing by, she felt constrained to silence. She finished by asking when she could go home.

'That depends on the Professor. He usually prefers to err on the side of caution, but tomorrow, all being well.' Grant smiled. 'I was speaking to your father. He would like you to go to Chatswood Gardens where there'll be someone to keep an eye on you. Will you do that?'

Anne nodded. 'For a few days . . . although I don't need looking after, do I? I'm not ill.'

'No, just a bit battered,' he returned, stroking her cheek with the back of his hand.

Later, when she sat out to have her bed made, Anne was surprised to discover how shaky she felt, and she was really quite glad to get back in and lie down again. Her head, though, had cleared a lot, and with the day staff busy with their last-minute routines before the end of their shift, Anne had plenty of time to dwell on her miraculous escape. It was a humbling experience, to be handed back your life, as it were.

With all her heart she wished that she could call back the last forty-eight hours. She bitterly regretted her petulance during and after the ball. Even if Grant didn't feel inclined to take a chance on her, at least he might still *like* her if she'd acted like a responsible adult instead of the spoiled brat he obviously thought she was. Behaving the way she had could well have ruined his life as well as her own.

She gave a resigned sigh. There was little point in agonising over the past. They hadn't died, or been badly injured, and she'd been given a chance to make amends. She'd been so blinkered, not even trying to understand *his* point of view. He'd been right to tell her she couldn't have everything she wanted, and if that was the way he felt she would have to accept it.

Being practical, she could always lose herself in her work. What a stupid idea it had been to think of giving up her course to avoid the pain of seeing him! Recalling some of those brave, trusting patients whose lives had briefly touched her own, she felt ashamed of her own lack of courage. What wouldn't some of them have given for a reprieve like hers? She would just meet things day by day and do the best she could.

Sara popped in for a moment to say goodnight when the day staff left. Alone again now, and with the ward lights dimmed, Anne once more found her thoughts revolving around her problems. She couldn't help being heartsick at Grant's rejection, but acceptance was the only way to salvage anything. If she could keep his friendship, that would be better than nothing.

Hearing movement nearby, she hastily dabbed at her moist eyes with a corner of the sheet and caught her trembling bottom lip between her teeth. The last person she expected to see at that time of night was Grant, casually dressed in navy cords and a sweatshirt, and looking unbearably lovable. He came to her bedside, a frown between his dark brows as he sensed her distress. 'What is it?' he asked, his concerned voice making matters worse. 'In pain, are you?'

'No, no . . . it's just . . .' she choked, and blurted out, 'Oh, Grant, I'm so sorry. Will you forgive me?'

'Forgive you?' He sat down beside her and took her hand in his. 'My darling girl, I'm the one who should be sorry. Dear God! I can't bear to think of how it might have turned out.'

She gave a long tremulous sigh of relief. It was

heaven just to be able to meet his eyes and know that he wasn't still mad with her. After a moment she lowered her lashes and faltered, 'Wh-what I really meant was, if I hadn't distracted you . . . picking that silly argument . . .'

'. . . the tramp would still have wandered into the road, and my reaction would still have been what it was,' he said reasonably. 'Anyway, it takes two to argue, so forget it.'

She half-smiled. 'If you'd stopped to slap my spoiled backside, as you threatened . . .'

Grant put his tongue in his cheek, then grinned. 'Saying is one thing, doing is another. I don't beat up women, although I admit I was sorely tempted.'

'You'd have got slapped back if you'd tried,' she said with a touch of her old spirit.

Grant chuckled. 'That's more like my Anne! Now, is there anything you want . . . anything I can get you?'

She shook her head. 'Except . . . perhaps . . . a top-up hug?'

'Your bruised ribs wouldn't enjoy that at all,' he reminded her. 'Just be patient.' Squeezing her hand, he stood up to leave. 'Now you go to sleep like a good girl. There's nothing to worry about—your progress is normal. And Anne . . .' bending down, he whispered close to her ear, 'I *do* love you.'

When he had gone she gazed after him, uncomprehending, scarcely able to believe what she'd heard. Was her brain still befogged? The *my darling girl* bit might have been a figure of speech, but he hadn't needed to say *I love you*. In any case, as he had pointed out, saying was one thing. It didn't imply that he intended to do anything about it. Before the crash he had told her he was more convinced than ever that things were impossible between them. Nothing had changed.

She gave up trying to fathom it out when the night staff nurse came to do her routine checks.

'My goodness, you're looking a bit more lively than you did last night,' the girl said. 'You had us all worried sick! Especially Ryder. I've never seen him so uptight before.'

'He must have been feeling responsible, I suppose,' said Anne, 'although the accident wasn't his fault. He couldn't have run the old boy down, could he? Must have been an unnerving experience . . .'

'Yeah, he was pretty white around the gills,' the nurse remembered. 'Night Sister had to practically force him to sit down and drink a cup of coffee. Thank goodness everything turned out all right, eh?'

Settling down to sleep, Anne decided to leave all her unanswered questions in the lap of the gods.

The following morning Grant was her first visitor, looking in before he started his outpatient clinic. 'Progress maintained?' he asked briskly, looking at her charts, feeling her pulse. 'Dear me, that's running on a bit!'

'You go away,' she said, 'and it'll settle down. I'm all right.'

He smiled and shook his head. 'Imagine all my tomorrows without a saucy come-back from you!

What a prospect! Think you'll be leaving today?'

'I hope so.'

He nodded. 'If I don't get up to see you before you go, take it easy, won't you? And any problems, report back stat. OK?'

'Mrs Mac will make sure that I do,' she smiled.

His bleep going at that moment cut short his visit. 'Damn,' he muttered. 'You be good now. So long,' and he strode off towards the telephone.

Professor Drapper cleared her for discharge that afternoon, with instructions to take some sick leave. She phoned Mrs Mac, who arrived in due course to collect her, and a taxi quickly bore them away to Kensington. Much as Anne had appreciated the care of her friends, she was not sorry to say goodbye and exchange the role of patient for the comforts of home.

It was pleasant to be mothered and made a fuss of for a time. She sat in the garden and idled the time away, dreaming hopeless, impossible dreams of if only . . .

Her Aunt Laura called with flowers, Brad sent flowers and Jonathan sent flowers. Mandy, Hazel and Sara came together to afternoon tea, and Mrs Mac bustled around enjoying having some young life in the old home again.

On Anne's second evening Michelle favoured them with her company, and they had dinner together with their father. It was as they finished their meal that Grant first rang to ask how she was.

'What about this young man, Anne?' her father enquired when they sat over coffee in the conservatory. 'He seems to be interested in you.'

'That was a professional follow-up,' she explained with a wry smile. 'I expect I'm on his conscience.'

'Well, if it should go any further than that, I should raise no objections,' said Sir Randolph. 'I like the fellow.'

Anne laughed. 'The trouble is, Daddy, he's the one raising objections, would you believe?'

Her father smiled. 'As a matter of fact it doesn't surprise me. Pride can be a bed of nails. Thought I'd let you know there'd be no problem so far as I'm concerned.'

'Phooey!' scoffed Michelle. 'Anne's trouble is she's too transparent. Play hard to get, darling, if you want him.'

'Is that what you are doing with the worthy American?' their father enquired drily.

Michelle wrinkled her pert nose at him. 'Maybe.'

He sighed and shook his head. 'I must admit, he seems a genuinely nice chap. Don't string him along.'

'Brad's no fool,' she said. 'We understand each other.'

By the next weekend time had begun to hang heavily for Anne. She still had a few more days of sick leave, but with nothing to do at Chatswood Gardens she felt unsettled and at a loose end. At length she decided it was time to go back to her own flat where at least there would be Mandy to talk to, and news of the hospital, and perhaps of

Grant.

'Well, if you must go,' her father said before
leaving for a round of golf on Saturday morning,
'get a taxi—I don't want you wandering around on
the Underground. I think you should take life
quietly for a little longer.'

After having morning coffee with Mrs Mac, she
went upstairs to pack and was about to call for a
taxi when Grant rang for the third time.

'How are you today . . . and what are you doing?'
he wanted to know.

Her heart began its usual clamour at the sound
of his voice. Their previous conversations had been
pleasant, chatty, but leading nowhere in particular.
Now she said, 'I'm fine, really. I'll be back at work
on Wednesday. I was just about to go back to the
flat.'

'Ah! Well, hold it, will you? I want to show you
my new car. May I come and pick you up?'

'That would be nice,' she returned, her moderate
manner totally at odds with the furore inside her.
'What have you got?'

'Nothing upmarket. Another Ford, but she's
great. All I need is a beautiful blonde sitting beside
me. I thought you might fill the bill very nicely.'

Anne laughed softly. 'Gee, thanks! Just needed
for decoration, am I?'

'That's something I'm not prepared to discuss on
the telephone. See you in half an hour.'

For the next thirty minutes Anne almost went
round in circles while she waited.

'That was Grant,' she told Mrs Mac, trying not

to show her excitement. 'He's just replaced his car and he's bringing it over to show me.' She looked down at her comfortable old jeans and primrose cotton shirt. 'I think I'll change,' she started to go up to her room, then paused. 'No, perhaps not. No point in dressing up just to go for a spin. Oh, maybe I will. These are a bit tatty . . . what do you think, Mac?'

The housekeeper laughed. 'You always look nice, whatever you wear, dear, but I like dresses myself.'

'OK, you've talked me into it.' Running up to her room, Anne exchanged jeans for a Liberty print cotton in bright summer colours, just in case Grant should suggest taking her to lunch.

Mrs Mac let him in and disappeared discreetly after showing him to the sitting-room.

Anne skipped down the stairs. 'Hi!' she said, beaming as she peered out of the window to see the new sapphire-blue car parked outside. 'You're pleased with it, are you?'

He didn't answer that. He simply held out his arms to her with an odd sort of smile on his face. 'Ready for that top-up now?'

'Mmm . . . just go a bit easy,' she returned, happy but utterly confused by a certain look in his compelling blue eyes.

He growled a bit. 'The way I'm feeling at this moment, that might be difficult.' He took her into a close embrace, and there was no laughter in his voice when he said, 'Anne . . . there's something I have to ask you.'

She was startled by his intensity. Her blood pounded in her ears. 'Yes, what's that?' she returned.

'Do you love me?'

She caught her breath, wincing a little as his arms tightened. 'I-I thought you'd know that,' she faltered. 'Michelle says I'm transparent.'

'Oh, my darling . . .' His seeking mouth found hers and his jubilant kisses filled her with a joy so great she felt like one enchanted.

Presently, when their lips parted for a moment, she shook her head in complete bewilderment. 'I-I don't understand this, Grant. Why am I now the flavour of the month?'

'You mean why have I suddenly come to my senses?' He pressed a gentle kiss on the fading bruise on her forehead. 'The thought of all my tomorrows without you had me climbing the wall. You always have been the flavour of the month, my love, but it was nearly losing you that showed me the folly of my ways. Time's too short to waste. Anne, will you have this misguided fool?'

Her hands reached into the dark waves at the back of his head. 'I might,' she teased in a vain attempt to follow her sister's advice, 'providing I'm not second best. What about that other girl you said had condemned you to a lonely old age?'

'That was you, dumbo,' he grinned, squeezing her a little so that she squeaked. 'Want to see if we can make it work?'

Her face was radiant. 'Oh, Grant, I promise you it will, if it's up to me.'

'You grabbed my heart from way back,' he murmured huskily. 'I must have been mad to deny it.' They kissed again, sweet kisses that transcended all barriers. Presently he said, his lips on her hair, 'Brad is at your sister's. Let's go and tell them the good news. I want the whole world to know.'

'Er . . . excuse me, what news is that?' Anne queried.

'That you're going to marry me.' Grant looked slightly nonplussed. 'What else?'

'I didn't know I'd been asked.'

He threw back his head and laughed. 'No half measures with me, my beloved. Either you marry me, or it's off. Well?'

'I will, I will, I will,' she said hastily. 'Don't stop kissing me or I'll think I've been dreaming.'

He waited just long enough to say, 'Listen, if your dreams are this erotic, I shall have to censor them. From now on we share everything, right?'

Then he kissed her again, fiercely, possessively, until she forgot bruised ribs in the heaven of being where she had always longed to be.

And in the quiet garden square, beyond the open windows, a blackbird sang its heart out, like a glorious fanfare to the triumph of love.

2 NEW TITLES FOR JANUARY 1990

Mariah *by Sandra Canfield is the first novel in a sensational quartet of sisters in search of love...* Mariah's sensual and provocative behaviour contrasts enigmatically with her innocent and naive appearance... Only the maverick preacher can recognise her true character and show her the way to independence and true love.

£2.99

Faye is determined to make a success of the farm she has inherited – but she hadn't accounted for the bitter battle with neighbour, Seth Carradine, who was after the land himself. In desperation she turns to him for help, and an interesting bargain is struck.

Kentucky Woman by Casey Douglas, bestselling author of Season of Enchantment. **£2.99**

W●RLDWIDE

Available from Boots, Martins, John Menzies, W.H. Smith, Woolworths and other paperback stockists.

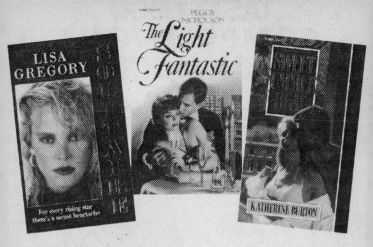

SOLITAIRE – Lisa Gregory   £3.50

Emptiness and heartache lay behind the facade of Jennifer Taylor's
glittering Hollywood career. Bitter betrayal had driven her to
become a successful actress, but now at the top, where else
could she go?

SWEET SUMMER HEAT – Katherine Burton   £2.99

Rebecca Whitney has a great future ahead of her until a sultry
encounter with a former lover leaves her devastated...

THE LIGHT FANTASTIC – Peggy Nicholson   £2.99

In this debut novel, Peggy Nicholson focuses on her own
profession... Award-winning author Tripp Wetherby's fear of
flying could ruin the promotional tour for his latest blockbuster.
Rennie Markell is employed to cure his phobia, whatever it takes!

These three new titles will be out in bookshops from February 1990.

W⦿RLDWIDE

*Available from Boots, Martins, John Menzies, W.H. Smith, Woolworths and other
paperback stockists.*

TASTY FOOD COMPETITION!

How would you like a years supply of Mills & Boon Romances ABSOLUTELY FREE? Well, you can win them! All you have to do is complete the word puzzle below and send it in to us by March. 31st. 1990. The first 5 correct entries picked out of the bag after that date will win **a years supply of Mills & Boon Romances** (*ten books every month - **worth £162**) What could be easier?

CLAM	HOLLANDAISE	OYSTERS	SPICE
COD	JAM	PRAWN	STEAK
CREAM	LEEK	QUICHE	TART
ECLAIR	LEMON	RATATOUILLE	
EGG	MELON	RICE	**PLEASE TURN OVER FOR DETAILS ON HOW TO ENTER**
FISH	MERINGUE	RISOTTO	
GARLIC	MOUSSE	SALT	
HERB	MUSSELS	SOUFFLE	

HOW TO ENTER

All the words listed overleaf, below the word puzzle, are hidden in the grid. You can find them by reading the letters forward, backwards, up or down, or diagonally. When you find a word, circle it or put a line through it, the remaining letters (which you can read from left to right, from the top of the puzzle through to the bottom) will ask a romantic question.

After you have filled in all the words, don't forget to fill in your name and address in the space provided and pop this page in an envelope (you don't need a stamp) and post it today. Hurry - competition ends March 31st 1990.

Mills & Boon Competition,
FREEPOST,
P.O. Box 236,
Croydon,
Surrey. CR9 9EL

Only one entry per household

Hidden Question _____

_____

Name _____

Address _____

_____

_____

_____ Postcode _____

You may be mailed with other offers as a result of this application.

MAILING
PREFERENCE
SERVICE

COMP 8